THE WISE FOLK of CHELM

THE WISE FOLK OF CHELM

SEYMOUR ROSSEL

Rossel Books
Houston, Texas

For further information contact:

Rossel Books
10114 Cliffwood Dr.
Houston, Texas 77035
www.rossel.net

ISBN 978-0-940646-42-1, cloth
ISBN 978-0-940646-43-8, paper
Library of Congress Control Number: 2013913147

DEDICATION

For **Sid & Sis Sherman** —
*What a privilege
to live and love and laugh
with you both. – SR*

Contents

PREFACE

❋ It is only through *chutzpah*—a mixture of impudence and audacity—that I present *The Wise Folk of Chelm*, a new rendition and conception of the veritable and venerable stories of Chelm. In my modest moments, I acknowledge that the Chelm tradition will survive in spite of what I do and regardless of your reception of my efforts. In my more arrogant moments, I feel I am breathing new life and new purpose into the comical pleasures of Chelm.

My Chelm is a tiny village at the end of a long road leading through the forest, seated behind a gated city wall, nestled at the base of a great mound the Chelmers call their mountain, and situated alongside a river that Chelmers have always claimed as the Chelm River. In all its particulars, it bears no resemblance to the historical Chelm. It is a place of legend, a Middle Earth of a kind—or even better, a Hobbiton—inhabited by unique folk distinguished not by their diminutive size or hairy feet but rather by their foolish insistence that any problem can be solved by the proper amount of applied group-think.

If you love good stories and enjoy smiling (and sometimes laughing), that may be all the introduction you need to *The Wise Folk of Chelm*. Nevertheless, you may be curious to know what motivated me to assay this work, and if so, I will briefly mount a shaky soapbox to let you in on what I was thinking and why I was willing to climb out on this limb

where so many worthy authors have preceded me (many suc-
cessfully).

Since the 1950s, most new Chelm stories have been written for children, often as showcases for the art of genuinely
talented illustrators. A few of the traditional Chelm stories
are particularly easy to adapt for children, so these tales tend
to appear and reappear with predictable regularity. Further-
more, most recent versions adopt the typical stance of eigh-
teenth and nineteenth century renditions namely, that the
canon of Chelm tales were 1) promulgated by Yiddish-speak-
ers from eastern Europe, 2) set in Poland (usually in Czarist
times), and 3) originally intended as a piquant means of cop-
ing with the vicissitudes of the anti-Semitism and grinding
poverty of the time.

Actually, Chelm stories circulated first among German
Jews in the sixteenth century purely as entertainment (adult
entertainment, at that). They were told by Jews who were not
particularly self-conscious or defensive about their status.
Nor were these German Jews especially poor. The early stories (later to be set in Chelm) were satiric but only in the
sense that they poked fun at ordinary foolishness. Nearly-
identical stories were simultaneously popular among non-
Jewish Germans (who had actually originated them and located them in a fictional town called Schildburg). Evidently,
Germans and Jews found the stories equally amusing.

In the course of authenticating my collection, *The Essen-
tial Jewish Stories* (2011), I researched the origins of Jewish
tales from numerous times and places. The few Chelm stories
I chose for that book raised my consciousness (as we moderns
like to say) and I felt impelled to attempt to restore Chelm's
original mythic mirth. The people you will meet in my Chelm
are my own creations. The stories you will read are told in my
own way, with my own twists and turns, and in a kind of us-
age that I describe as "slapstick narrative" or "narrative slapstick." And yet my Chelm is authentic to its classic core, as
you will soon discover.

If you crave a bit of pure unadulterated grownup fun, *The Wise Folk of Chelm* is for you. Enjoy.

Seymour Rossel
Houston, Texas
August 9, 2013

❀ The author would like to thank Lorna Keating for her excellent proofreading and incisive suggestions. My appreciation, too, to friends who read the manuscript and made useful observations—the redoubtable Rabbi Manuel Gold, the sagacious and discerning Rabbi Sheldon Zimmerman, and the perspicacious David Behrman of Behrman House, Inc.; to my daughters Rabbi Amy Rossel Ross, Deborah Rossel Bradford, and Rabbi Rachel M. Maimin; and to my son Benjamin Maimin. And special thanks are due to my wife, Sharon L. Wechter, who read and reread the manuscript and shared her invariably valuable insights. - *SR*

THE WISE FOLK OF CHELM

HOW THE TOWN OF CHELM CAME TO BE

❃ It is written in the Holy Books that whenever God speaks, an angel is created. And, since God always speaks with a purpose, every angel is a messenger with its own purpose. Two angels do not share the same task; nor can one angel have more than one task. From this we learn that the number of God's angels is as countless as the stars in the heavens. As it is said, "Over every blade of grass, every herb of the field, every flower, and every leaf of every tree, an angel stands whispering, 'Grow, grow. Grow and prosper.'"

God created human beings in God's image. Not in God's physical image, of course, since God has no physical image. We are created in the image of God the Creator, for we are creators, too. Just as God imagines things and brings them into being, we imagine things and bring them into being. Thus, God created human beings and gave them minds and placed angels over each of them, and every person's angel whispers, "Grow!" and "Prosper!"—even "Learn!" and "Be wise!" God wished the best for every human being.

This is important information, and without it we cannot understand the beginning of the strange and beguiling tale of the wise folk of the village of Chelm. Their story begins with a problem:

You see, some human beings were content to grow and prosper and study and create new things. But some human beings were lazy. (Human beings created laziness, of course, almost right from the start.) They refused to learn and saw no

1

great problem in creating things without thinking through what would be the end of their creations. Without wisdom, they soon created lying, cheating, and bullying; and these led them to create greed and envy, strife and war. It was not long before God heard the painful sounds of people suffering.

God watched and waited. After all, some human beings were discovering the joys of wisdom; they created farms and villages, arts and crafts, dancing and singing, and schools and academies. Perhaps, God thought, the wiser ones would teach their neighbors to turn away from laziness, greed, and strife. Of course, you know what really happened. Things went from bad to worse and beyond. God told Noah to build a great ship. After the flood, God thought, "Now, surely, human beings have learned their lesson. They are free to begin again!"

The flood was only an intermission. In no time at all, human beings spread across the earth and reinvented laziness and foolishness. God sought a new solution. "Perhaps," thought God, "it would help if the number of wise souls were greater than the number of foolish souls." God spoke twice and two angels came into being.

One angel was given the task of gathering up wise souls from places where too many wise folk had gathered and taking them to where there were too many lazy and callous folk. If this angel were successful, there would be wise folk, good teachers, and good organizers in every community.

The other angel was set the task of gathering up foolish souls from places where there were too many foolish souls. "Return the foolish souls to Me," God charged the angel, "and I will repair them."

Who can say which task was more difficult? Look around. How many wise people do you see? Wise folk are as precious as diamonds, as treasured as nuggets of purest gold. And like gold and diamonds, the wise are rare and hard to find. But when it comes to foolish souls, you hear about them day and night. They are like the sand on the shore of the sea and their foolishness is more contagious than the measles.

For years, the first angel searched for wise souls. Here and there, a single one was found and had to be left in place. Only occasionally, too many wise men were gathered together in one place—you could tell because they had taken to arguing and bickering. The angel would swoop down and throw all but one of these wise souls into her sack. Then she would fly to a place where wise folk were needed and set the wise souls among them.

As for the other angel, her problem was that so many foolish souls could be gathered in a day that just scooping them up and returning them to heaven for repair was a consuming task. As soon as her bag was full of foolish souls she would fly to heaven, deposit the souls, and return for another bagful.

Unfortunately, angels are not perfect. They make mistakes just as human beings do. That may be the reason for what went wrong. Or, perhaps, some of the foolishness of the foolish souls rubbed off on the angel as she made so many trips each day carrying so many fools to heaven. Who can say? Either way, the angel bethought herself an idea destined to backfire. Every time she reached heaven, she grabbed a larger sack than the one she had carried before. The larger the sack, she reasoned, the more foolish souls would fit in it and the less trips she would have to make back and forth.

This worked; that is, until she grabbed a sack that was far too big. She filled it with foolish souls and had trouble even lifting it to her shoulder. That was her first warning. With the sack across her shoulder, she had trouble taking off. That was her second warning. Moreover, the slightest breeze was enough to slow down her upward journey. That was the third and final warning. And that is when it happened:

She was flying much too close to the ground when she came to a tall hill capped by pine trees. She struggled to fly over the top of the hill when a sudden gust of wind hit her. It was just enough to topple her over. It was just enough to cause her to lose her hold on the bag. It was just enough to blow the bag against the pine trees where needles and cones made quick work of ripping the bag to shreds.

Out poured the largest collection of foolish souls ever gathered in one place on the face of the earth. Every one of them hit the ground rolling, tipping, tumbling, and careening to the bottom of the hill. Lo and behold, nestled between the hill and the river was the innocent town of Chelm, a place where people had never been either too wise or too foolish. That is, until now, when the tumbling souls, glad to find a journey's end, each seized one of the villagers and inhabited him or her.

Suddenly, the town of Chelm was transformed. Since everyone was now foolish, the Chelmers looked at one another and immediately recognized the same amount of wisdom in the face they were seeing as they believed they had. So the foolish conclusion reached by each and every one of the Chelmers was the exact same at the exact same moment: Every one of them, they surmised, was wise. Indeed, the whole town brimmed to the full with wisdom the like of which none of them had ever known before. Indeed, it was wisdom the like of which would never be known again, either.

Pity the poor angel. She sped upward to Heaven to report the bad news. How afraid she was to face her Creator! But she was brave enough to stand and relate what had happened. She was wise enough to make one apology after another. She was canny enough to suggest that she could clear the problem up in only a few days' time by making a few trips down and up with a normal size bag. Suddenly, she realized that she was speaking non-stop and had been doing so for quite a little while.

God said, "Not to worry, little one. I know it was an accident and you are forgiven. But as the humans say, 'Sometimes fortune smiles.' I think we will leave the souls where they are and see what happens. Whatever happens, it is certain to be a great deal of fun to watch."

And that, or so the legend goes, is how the town of Chelm came to be.

THE NEW RABBI OF CHELM

❋ Reb Feivel, the new rabbi of Chelm, was a man of habits. What happened to the old rabbi is another story.

To become a rabbi, Feivel attended the famous *yeshiva* in Lvov. The famous rabbis who ran the famous yeshiva were deeply impressed by Feivel's habits. In accordance with advice passed down from the ancient sages, the famous rabbis instructed their students to "choose a teacher and deserve a companion." So the hopeful scholars sat scattered through the study room in pairs. The procedure hardly varied from pair to pair. Imagine a sample case, as the Talmud does, by calling one mock student Ploni and the other Almoni.

Ploni would read a passage and Almoni would repeat it in his own words. Almoni would read the next passage and Ploni would phrase it in his own words. Back and forth, forth and back they went. Meanwhile, it was customary for both Ploni and Almoni to read and reiterate to one another in a kind of sing-song chanting, on the theory that what was sung was more readily remembered than what was merely spoken. This time-tested method is known far and wide as *chevruta*, "companionship."

Each companion had his favorite chant and no two sing-song recitations were alike. The crowded study room was thus a constant cacophony of sound. In the midst of this din, Feivel demonstrated his most persistent habit. He would fall asleep an instant after sitting down, leaving his partner to shrug his shoulders and continue to chant from the Holy

7

Books in sing-song. To this, Feivel answered occasionally, with a snore.

The famous rabbis of Lvov all agreed that Feivel's habit of falling asleep was beyond doubt his most impressive trait. Not that they were not also impressed by his habit of upending human logic. For example, when a student seemed ready, after studying a page of Talmud or a weekly portion from the Torah, the famous rabbis would call him near and quiz him on what he had studied. When they called on Feivel, he reported to their table and sat before them. The rabbis asked one question after another and Feivel knew the answer to not a single one.

"Thank you," Feivel would say. "Now I am ready to study."

One of the famous rabbis pulled at the corners of his beard and ventured, "Before you came to be tested, you were not ready to study?"

"Of course not," Feivel replied. "Before you called on me, I did not know the questions. How could I know the answers before I knew the questions?"

Another of the famous rabbis inquired, "You wait to know the questions before you study?"

Feivel nodded. "Most assuredly," he said. "It is my habit to know the questions so that I can study to know the answers."

Another of the famous rabbis queried, "And if we change the questions when you come back with your answers?"

"Aha!" said Feivel. "That is what makes my habit so useful. All I have to do then is go back and study until I get those answers."

Armed with the questions, Feivel returned to his partner and an instant later was heard to reply to a sing-song oration with a particularly nasal snore. Looking on, the famous rabbis of Lvov threw up their hands. They held a conference, arguing and debating for an hour. Afterward, they sent a pupil to awaken Feivel.

When Feivel was before them again, the eldest rabbi addressed him. "We are impressed by your habits—so impressed that we think you are ready now to leave the yeshiva."

"But I want to become a rabbi," Feivel responded, knowing that studying to become a rabbi could take a long time.

The eldest of the famous rabbis nodded. "So you said when you came to us last week. And we think you will be pleased by our decision.

"The world is a big place," the eldest rabbi went on, "and different parts of it have different needs. Most places require a rabbi who has studied a long time and can repeat what he knows on command. But there is one place in the world that is ready for you, one place where your habits will be the epitome of wisdom."

"You will like it there," said another of the famous rabbis. "In distance, it is close by; in spirit, it is a world apart. We are sending you to Chelm to replace their old rabbi and become their new rabbi."

"Chelm?" Feivel hesitated. "I have never heard of it."

"Better and better," said the eldest rabbi.

"But what happened to their old rabbi?" Feivel asked.

"That's another story altogether," said the eldest rabbi as he raised one hand up in the air and gestured significantly in the direction of Heaven. He stood, came around the table, and placed his hands on Feivel's head. "You have my blessing to be the rabbi of Chelm," he said.

One by one, each of the other famous rabbis came and laid hands on Feivel's head. "To Chelm, with my blessing," said one. "May you and Chelm be a perfect fit," said another. "You have my blessing to stay in Chelm," said the last. All the while, the eldest rabbi pulled at his beard and nodded his head. At the end, he probed, "Do you have any last questions, Reb Feivel?"

Feivel thought for a moment before answering. "Only one: What became of Chelm's old rabbi?"

"Never mind," said the eldest rabbi, and all the famous rabbis of the yeshiva of Lvov intoned in unison, "That's another story."

THE GLORY OF CHELM

❀ Sabbath ends when the sun goes down, and Jews everywhere praise God for separating light from darkness, the holy from the mundane, and the one day of rest from the six days of labor. In Chelm, they also praise God for separating the fools from the wise.

Most Chelmers hurry home at sundown to eat their dinner, but it was Reb Feivel's habit at the close of the Sabbath to take a long walk. He often climbed part way up the stately hill that Chelmers called their mountain. From here, he could look down on the village and its ramshackle wooden houses lit from within by the flickering of candlelight so that they looked below like a reflection of the great sky above with its myriad stars.

He sat beneath a tree and studied the twinkling above him and the twinkling below him. And, as was his wont, as he studied, he dozed off. When he awoke, he was lying flat on his back and looking up through the branches of the trees. He saw the moon and thought:

"Moon, O Moon, how wondrous are you among God's many works! You shine with majesty and brilliance, a thousand times more brightly than the brightest star! You were created on the same day as the sun. You give light just as the sun gives light. But your light, O Moon, is even more important than the light of the sun. The sun is nearly superfluous, for it lights the daytime when we hardly need it. By day, the world is bright and we can already see clearly all that sur-

11

rounds us. The wonder of your light, O Moon, comes by night when it is dark so that you are a lamp for our feet and a beacon for our eyes. Moon, O Moon, how wondrous you are!"

Thinking these deep thoughts, he looked up and almost panicked. He was shocked to discover that the crescent moon—in its last quarter, so that it resembled nothing more than the horns of a bull—had gotten tangled in the branches of the tree above his head.

"This will never do," he thought. "I must rouse myself and get help. I must run to Chelm and fetch a few young men to climb the tree and shake the moon loose. We must not allow the moon to remain trapped this way."

Nothing, however, is gained by rushing to do before thinking things through. So he lay still, trying to determine how many young men it would take to make the human ladder that would be necessary to reach the lower branches of the tall tree, how many men would have to climb the human ladder in order to ascend to the topmost branches of the tree's crown, and how many hands would be necessary to shake the top branches to set free the moon. As always, with Reb Feivel, thinking had its price. He fell into a deep sleep.

He dreamed he saw a human ladder, made up of the men of Chelm, stretching from earth to Heaven. The women of Chelm were ascending and descending the ladder, carrying rags and pails. On the way up, the women's rags were white as the feathers of doves. On the way down, the rags were as dark as raven feathers. Looking up, he saw why. The women of Chelm were polishing the moon. Already they had polished it so that you could see half its shining disk; and soon they would polish it so that, though it had been just a crescent when they started, it would be at its full glory and brighter than it had been in ages! What angels were these women of Chelm! And how mighty the men of Chelm who stood steadfast and strong, one upon another's shoulders, a human stairway to Heaven!

In his dream, he heard a heavenly voice saying, "Come look, Reb Feivel. Thanks to the wisdom of the townsfolk of Chelm, from now on every night will be bright and clear. Every night the moon will be full. And the peoples of all the earth will praise the town of Chelm and its worthy rabbi for your work will be a blessing to all the nations."

Just then, Reb Feivel awakened with a tremendous shudder to the sound of his own snoring. Looking up, he panicked again. The moon had disappeared! He had lain too long thinking instead of running to town to get help. He started to rise, but noticed as he turned over that he was wrong. There in the distance he saw the horned moon beyond the trees and beyond the mountain of Chelm.

"So," he thought, "the moon escaped from the tree without my help this time." Then he thought, "I am hungry. I had better return to Chelm before I fall asleep again." Then he thought, "But I had better mark this spot where I was sleeping, so that the next time the moon gets trapped in this tree, I will know where to bring the young men of Chelm." He looked around and found twelve goodly stones and piled them up in a little pyramid to make a marker pointing up to the branches.

The next day, Reb Feivel attended the meeting of the council of the elders of Chelm, a baker's dozen of the wisest of the wise. Tzeitel the Butcher's Wife was there, famous for her knowledge of bones and sinew, always ready with a cutting remark. Yankel the Tailor was there, renowned for his skill in stitching ideas together. The three sages of the academy of Chelm were there, each famous for his own invention in the art of thinking. Also present were Zalman Shelomo, Chelm's gatekeeper; the wise Sissel, renowned for her sweet and peerless *tzimmes* (a concoction of slowly simmered fruit and vegetables) and for making a tzimmes of almost anything; Kalman the Fixer, widely known for tinkering with metals, woods, and ideas; Zelig the Bedecked, the mayor of Chelm; Zev the Treasurer of Chelm; Naftali the Water Carrier, and his counterpart, Hirschel the Wood Carrier, and Raisel the Matchmaker.

Reb Feivel told the elders of the moon caught in the tree, the dream, and all that transpired on the mountain of Chelm. When he was finished, he sat down. The elders sat in rapt attention. They appeared stunned, speechless.

Zelig the Bedecked, mayor of Chelm, rose at last. He cleared his throat and it seemed he was about to speak, but instead he began to clap.

The whole company jumped up and joined him in a hearty round of applause. Smiles spread across every face and Sissel swore to herself that she would repeat the rabbi's story in the hen house as soon as possible so that all the women who came to pick eggs for their recipes would hear of it. The women would tell one another and also tell their men. The story would spread by the riverside where women came to do their laundry. It would spread in the synagogue where men gathered to pray. It would spread in the Monday market and the Thursday market. It would spread at the *mikveh* where townsfolk came to purify themselves for the Sabbath. It would spread throughout Chelm.

Zelig the Bedecked motioned for silence. One by one, the elders resumed their seats. Now he spoke, "We must be the envy of every town. Certainly, it is now confirmed. There could not be a finer fit."

At the word "fit," Yankel the Tailor stood and exclaimed, "Tailor-made! A fit tailor-made!"

"Thank you, Yankel," said the mayor. "It is true. We are blessed by a rabbi whose wits match our own. And, since he is still young, you will see: His wisdom will continue to grow and he will be the very glory of Chelm in his old age."

Tzeitel rose. "Mayor," she said, "have we not agreed never to speak of rabbis and old age in a single breath?"

Many heads nodded in agreement.

The mayor said, "True. What I meant to say, of course, was 'in his advanced years.' He will be the glory of Chelm in his advanced years."

Tzeitel clucked. She hardly approved of this phraseology any better.

Raisel the Matchmaker stood to speak. "Let us not quibble about when. Let us declare Reb Feivel 'the Glory of Chelm' now and not wait. Why tinker with destiny?"

A few more remarks and a vote was taken. Reb Feivel was declared the Glory of Chelm. And so the matter might have remained, except for Reb Feivel.

"What about the moon?" he asked. "Can we ignore the advice of Heaven?"

Zev the Treasurer rose. "Surely, no wise man would ever ignore the advice of Heaven. But Heaven's advice in a dream... well, that's another matter entirely."

"True," said one of the sages from the academy of Chelm. "Even the Holy Books are of mixed opinion when it comes to dreams. It is written in the Talmud, 'Neither a good dream nor a bad dream is ever fully fulfilled.'" Upon which the sage placed his thumb in the air and waved it. "It is also written that 'A dream not interpreted is like a letter unread.'" Upon which he waved his thumb from side to side.

Zalman Shelomo the Gatekeeper rose to his feet. "I, for one, would not want to be part of a human ladder, tottering on someone else's shoulders just so some women can go climbing over me."

There was a kind of uneasy silence. Perhaps the wise elders were taking stock. Zalman Shelomo was larger than many an ox. There was little chance that any male of Chelm would allow him to be somewhere in the midst of a human ladder, and even less chance that any female of Chelm would attempt to clamber over the accumulated overhang of his belly.

Kalman was the first to recover. He proposed that the elders should discuss this knotty problem: How to honor

Heaven and not dishonor the Glory of Chelm, Reb Feivel. Perhaps there was some truth in the rabbi's dream and, if so, in all the world none were as qualified to ascertain the truth as the elders of Chelm.

So Zelig the Bedecked, the mayor of Chelm, sent for food, and the elders of Chelm discussed the matter for seven days and seven nights. They settled on the following:

Whereas, Heaven has called on Chelm to burnish the moon so that it can shine in its full glory not only for a short time each month but for every night of every month; and

Whereas, Reb Feivel himself (the Glory of Chelm) has witnessed the fact that the moon can be caught; and

Whereas, Chelm desires to do the work of Heaven.

Now Therefore, be it resolved that Chelm shall capture the moon, polish it until it shines as it did when it was fashioned by its Creator, and return it to the heavens to light the night.

Moreover, they agreed on a practical plan for trapping the moon. Naftali the Water Carrier testified that he had seen the moon when it was vulnerable to capture. Not only did it shine in the sky beyond human reach, but it also trailed through bodies of water, shining in the river, in barrels of rainwater, even in puddles on a stormy night. Catch it in the water and the plan would work! All the elders agreed. All of them had seen the moon just this way.

But water was not good enough for the moon. The people of Chelm could surely afford better. Was Chelm not justly proud of its plum spirits, its homegrown schnapps? Distilled and purified, plum schnapps was the epitome of clarity. Surely, the moon would be better tempted by schnapps than by mere water!

Avrom the Barrel Maker was put to work manufacturing an extraordinarily large barrel. Reb Feivel supervised, checking the staves and the hoops, ensuring the top was a tight fit. Within a month all was ready. The barrel was filled three-quarters of the way to the brim with Chelm's pride, plum liquor, manufactured in large enough quantity for this special purpose.

The whole town turned out for the momentous moment. For two nights, clouds covered the sky so that the moon was little more than a passing glow. But on the third night the moon appeared just as it had for Reb Feivel on the occasion of his dream: a crescent. On this night, the moon cleared the pines atop the mountain and made its way along the river until, lo and behold, it shone directly into the barrel.

"Quickly!" yelled Naftali, but Avrom was even quicker, clapping the top on the barrel and nailing it shut. The barrel was carefully lifted to a cart and pushed into the blacksmith shop. The next night, there was no moon in the sky. Lo, it was true! Behold, the moon was in the barrel. Chelm had captured the moon!

Part two of the plan now came into play. In the morning, the women of Chelm came with their rags and pails, ready to polish the moon. Everyone crowded into the blacksmith shop and the doors were closed to darken the room. Zelig the Bedecked stood close to the barrel and Reb Feivel stood beside him. Avrom and Yankel removed the nails, and a hush came over the townsfolk as the top was slowly lifted from the barrel.

What a shock of disappointment passed like a shudder through the people of Chelm. The moon was gone!

Sissel cried out in agony, "Thief! Thief!"

But Reb Feivel was a man of faith. "I think the moon has sunk to the bottom of the barrel," he announced.

"Of course," the mayor said. "That has to be the explanation."

Tzeitel said, "Then, let us pour out the liquor and catch the moon in our hands so we can clean it."

Zalman Shelomo threw up his hands. "This is the way a woman reasons!" he said. "No man would just pour out the schnapps on the ground. You are talking about good plum liquor!"

Kalman the Fixer slapped Zalman Shelomo on the back. "The big man is wise," he said. "Let us repair to our homes and bring glasses. We will drink our way to the bottom of this barrel. Soon, we will reach the moon."

All day long, the people of Chelm dipped and drank, drank and dipped. Their serious task awaited them. In the meantime, the barrel was large and the amount of schnapps that had to be consumed was great. There was a lot of merriment and camaraderie, a lot of laughing and jesting, a lot of husbands nudging their wives, and a lot of wives jostling their husbands. Even people who normally would not talk to one another were hugging and chatting away like old friends.

Now Reb Feivel recalled how the moon had been caught in the branches of a tree. And he remembered how it had managed to slip out of the branches of the tree without any help. He was snoring when the last cup was dipped in the schnapps, when the people of Chelm reached the bottom of the barrel. But he would not have been surprised to learn that the moon had somehow escaped.

The main thing is, everyone went home fulfilled.

In time, the moon returned to the sky, and to the river, and to the puddles; and the people of Chelm were satisfied to see it return. As for Reb Feivel, the dreamer, he remained "the Glory of Chelm."

THE TZEDAKAH BOX

❈ Chelm had one baker and one tailor, one rabbi and one matchmaker, one blacksmith and one *shammes*—the redoubtable assistant to the rabbi who was also the caretaker of the synagogue. But Chelm had more than one person in many of its other roles: farmers, water carriers, dairymen, draymen, beekeepers, fixers, woodcutters, shepherds, and shopkeepers. This condition gave rise to a standing jest repeated by people in towns other than Chelm.

As the story goes, once there was a murder in Chelm and the tailor was brought to trial. Witnesses were called and testimony given. The tailor had murdered a customer who claimed that the jacket fashioned for him might fit a child or even a medium-sized goat, but it certainly did not fit him. The tailor's wife was called to the stand and admitted that it had been a hard day for the tailor. She owned up to the fact that she had berated him all morning in sharp tones. And her mother, who had recently come to live with them, had joined in the tongue-lashing. But, she said, they had meant no harm. Others who visited the shop that morning testified that Zelda and her mother Layla were not only shrill, but artful in both sarcasm and scorn, and the tailor surely appeared to have reached the limit of his patience. Just then, the unfortunate customer stormed in to the shop to complain. While others watched in horror, the customer threw his newly-fashioned jacket to the floor, stepped on it as if it were a rug, and commenced to stomp on it. Was the tailor unaware that he had his iron in his hand as he bent down to pick up the jacket? Did he realize when he pulled the jacket that he would cause the customer to tumble backward? As he reached out toward the customer, did he know that iron and customer would collide? Did he really mean to leave the customer dead and bleeding on the floor where the jacket had been? The judge asked each question slowly. But the poor tailor only shook his head and bent his body forward, muttering something to the effect that he knew not what he had intended. He was angry and wished he had stayed in bed that day. The judge ordered that justice be done: the tailor should be taken out and hanged.

The people of Chelm cried out. How could the judge be so unfeeling, so unthinking? What would people do when their clothing needed mending or when they wanted alterations? In all of Chelm there was only one tailor! How dare the judge command that the only tailor in town be hanged?

Now, one of the Chelmers approached the bench and offered a suggestion, "Your honor," he said, "it is true that there is only one tailor in Chelm, but we do have two butchers." The room was suffused with the sound of a collective affirmation. The judge said, "I see your point. My decision is that the tailor should continue to suffer from his mother-in-law and his wife, but to serve justice for the murder, let one of Chelm's butchers be hanged!"

Anyone in Chelm could tell you that none of this ever happened. For one thing—according to official town records—there never was a murder in Chelm. For another thing, Chelm had no judge; when necessary, the rabbi served. Last but not least, in truth, Chelm had only one butcher. So, you see, this tale of misadventure was only one of many similar canards about Chelm told only in surrounding towns, towns inhabited mainly by fools. For our part, we will avoid telling such outright myths. The true stories of Chelm are far more edifying.

Therefore, let us return to counting off the important facts of Chelm's occupations. Chelm had a rich man (who had a rich wife), a beggar (whose wife was apparently, but not actually, poor), and a thief (who was unmarried, as far as anyone knew). Gedaliah was the thief (and since the word for thief in Yiddish is *goniff*, he was known to all as Gedaliah the Goniff). The poor folk of Chelm (the vast majority) considered it a mark of distinction to have a resident thief. Due to the art of being poor, which is to live without much of value, Gedaliah was often idle. Then again, from time to time, he would find something worthy of his trade. Of course, if he were caught in the act, he would be brought to justice. But in a town entirely populated by wise folk, the thief was himself a wise fellow, and his handiwork was generally surmised, but not observed.

For example, as the new rabbi and the shammes were preparing the synagogue for the High Holy Days, Reb Feivel noticed that the old *tzedakah* box was worn out; indeed, it looked as if mice had chewed it top, bottom, and sides. The box was mounted shoulder-high on the wall beside the synagogue entrance so that those who entered could easily slip in a coin or two for the Tzedakah Fund. These coins were duly collected and saved as stipends for orphans and widows, to tide over those who lost their employment, and to provide small dowries for brides in need. Being a thoroughly modern sort, Reb Feivel knew that a more attractive tzedakah box would attract more charity funds. He raised just this point at a meeting of the elders.

The elders agreed and commissioned Ansel the Tinsmith to fashion a new tzedakah box in wood and tin. The new box was completed two weeks before the High Holy Days and was duly installed on the western wall beside the synagogue door. For the first two days after its installation, Reb Feivel, sitting at his chair along the eastern wall, smiled each time he heard the clink of a coin being dropped into the box. But on the third day, as the morning service began, Reb Feivel was dismayed because there was no clink at all. He was more dismayed when it was reported by the shammes that the new tzedakah box had vanished during the night. Reb Feivel visited the western wall and saw for himself the terrible truth: The new tzedakah box was nowhere to be seen.

The elders of Chelm were called. They filed by the synagogue entrance to see for themselves. It was immediately assumed that the villain who had stolen the new tzedakah box was none other than Gedaliah the Goniff.

Tzeitel the Butcher's Wife offered the first curse: "That thief should only live like a chandelier—hanging by day and burning by night!"

Sissel the Tzimmes Maker said, "Better they should free a madman and lock up this thief in his stead!"

Zelig the Bedecked, the mayor of Chelm, intoned, "For this blackguard, one misfortune is one too few!"

Raisel the Matchmaker said, "It should come to pass that this villain marries the daughter of the Angel of Death!"

And Zalman Shelomo, Chelm's gatekeeper, concluded, "I pray that I should outlive him, just long enough, that is, to bury him!"

So there it stood—an empty space formerly occupied by the new tin and wood tzedakah box and with no proof that it was Gedaliah the Goniff who had purloined it in the night.

Zelig said, "We must commission another tzedakah box at once."

Zev the Treasurer of Chelm cleared his throat. "Oy! The town treasury is low enough in funds. What if the goniff steals the next box, and the one after that?"

This conjecture caused a general commotion, and the elders began talking all at once. As usual, the discourse, the debate, and the thinking encompassed the next few days and nights. Food was brought in. Eventually, though, wisdom prevails in Chelm.

It was Kalman the Fixer who offered the salient suggestion, "The next tzedakah box should be fitted with a sign," he proffered, "and the sign should read, 'THIS TZEDAKAH BOX BELONGS TO THE PEOPLE OF CHELM.'"

"It's good. It's good," said the mayor. And the commission was again given to Ansel the Tinsmith who brought into being, in record time—just a few days—a beautiful new box with the shining sign on its front, composed in large, clear, unmistakable letters.

Kalman the Fixer was just about to affix the box to the western wall in its accustomed place when Reb Feivel stayed his hand.

"Is it enough?" the rabbi asked. "Will the sign alone stop the thief? After all, the last tzedakah box also belonged to the people of Chelm."

"True. True," said Zelig the Bedecked.

Yankel the Tailor spoke from his heart, "The wisdom of Kalman remains a lamp in the dark. We need the sign. But the wisdom of our rabbi is also incisive. To keep the tzedakah box safe from the thief, we need something more. We should hang the box from the ceiling, high up beside the chandelier, where the thief cannot reach it."

There was instant agreement. "Leave it to me," said Kalman. "By morning, I shall have the box so high that no thief could reach it."

And so it was when the elders convened in the synagogue the following morn. And, as surely as oil flows, the elders were proud of their collective work. The mayor turned to the treasurer and demanded a silver coin. He took the coin and presented it to Reb Feivel, saying, "You, our dear rabbi, the Glory of Chelm, should have the honor of placing the first coin in our new tzedakah box."

Reb Feivel received the coin with a brief word of thanks. (Brief, that is, in rabbinic terms, since it required twenty minutes in its delivery.) Then he looked up to the ceiling and realized that not only he, but no living soul, could reach that box to deposit a coin. Truth be told, in such cases, it was Reb

Feivel's habit to groan. And a long, grinding groan was all he could manage.

Zalman Shelomo, however, remembering the ladder in Reb Feivel's dream, said, "Be comforted, dear rabbi. This is no problem. Give me a moment to fetch the ladder we used to hang the box. The ladder will reach from floor to ceiling so that anyone making a donation will be able to drop his or her coin into the box."

Now, you can be certain that this is a true story because the selfsame ladder stands in the center of the synagogue of Chelm to this very day, a tribute to the wisdom of the elders of Chelm. Unfortunately, the tzedakah box itself went missing shortly after the High Holy Days. Thereafter, donations to Chelm's Tzedakah Fund were made directly to the shammes who regularly stands by the entrance at the western wall of the synagogue; and I am pleased to report that, as of the time of this writing, the shammes himself has not yet been stolen.

TO CATCH A THIEF

❀ Once, Reb Fishel, the richest man in Chelm (who was not a rabbi, but was called "Reb" as a sign of respect for his riches—though, it was understood, not for himself as a person), happened to bump into Gedaliah the Goniff.

"Excuse me, Reb Fishel," said Gedaliah, as he brushed any dust that might have been caused by the slight collision from Reb Fishel's jacket. "I hope you have a pleasant day."

Reb Fishel harrumphed, for he thought this was the proper way for a wealthy man to respond to the likes of Gedaliah the Goniff. And he watched Chelm's only professional thief calmly walking away. Then he turned and went into the tobacconist's shop to buy some snuff. But when he reached for his coin purse, he realized that the bumping into had not been an accident, and the brushing had been a manipulation. His pocket had been picked! His purse was gone like the breeze!

He ran out into the street, yelling, "Stop that thief! Catch that [Ed. Note: *The word he used here should not be replicated in print but—and you who know will instantly know—it denotes a fatherless individual*]!"

Now, the closest thing that Chelm has to a policeman is the formidable gatekeeper, Zalman Shelomo, who, on account of his girth, is not the fastest men in Chelm. Nevertheless, he soon crossed the town square and stood before Reb Fishel. The tale was told, and Zalman Shelomo promised to catch Gedaliah the Goniff and see that he got what was coming to him.

It was not many days before Zalman Shelomo found himself face to face with Gedaliah. At once, he grabbed the thief by his arm and shouted, "Ha! I have got you now. And I mean to see that you go to jail for stealing Reb Fishel's purse."

The thief shrugged.

"What have you to say for yourself?"

"Oh," said Gedaliah, "you have caught me fair and square. I suppose I must go with you."

Zalman Shelomo escorted his prisoner to the jail at the back of the Town Hall. Really, calling it a jail may be a bit of a stretch. With only one professional thief and no record of any murder, most disturbances were domestic complaints. Sometimes a Chelmer was accused of allowing his goat to eat a bit too freely on another Chelmer's blackberry bushes. Or a Chelmer might be accused of roasting a chicken that rightfully belonged to her neighbor. Minor offences were the rule. For the likes of these, the Chelm town jail sufficed.

The jail, entirely outdoors, consisted of a wooden box on which the prisoner was required to sit. The prisoner would face the fence where two wide holes had been opened. The prisoner was required to place his or her hands through the two holes. On the other side of the fence, the jailer would hand the prisoner a barrel hoop and the prisoner was required to hold it with both hands, thus rendering him or her helpless to move. At meal times, the prisoner had the choice of dining alfresco or repairing to the Town Hall to eat with the mayor, the treasurer, and other town officials. Of course, in case of rain or snow, the prisoner was brought indoors for a warming glass of tea laced with a little plum jam. As it was, the town beggar or his wife would, in the case of weeks when there was little charity available, arrange to find excuses to go to jail.

Zalman Shelomo instructed Gedaliah to be seated on the wooden box. That was all the instruction that Gedaliah the

Goniff required. He stretched his hands through the two openings in the fence and held the hoop with both hands to secure him from leaving. Zalman Shelomo, however, was taking no chances with this prisoner.

"Do you promise to stay here while I go to fetch the mayor and the rabbi?" he inquired.

"Oh," Gedaliah replied, "you have caught me fair and square."

Zalman Shelomo nodded in agreement. "I will be back in a little while," he said as he turned to go.

True to his word, Zalman Shelomo fetched the mayor and the rabbi, and, proud of his unprecedented capture of the thief, escorted them behind the Town Hall. The fence was there, the holes were there, the barrel hoop was there, but Gedaliah the Goniff was nowhere in sight.

"It seems," said the mayor, "that the prisoner has escaped."

"So it seems," said the rabbi.

"Evidently, a thief's word cannot be trusted," said Zalman Shelomo. "I shall know better next time."

"Yes," said the rabbi, "but will there be a next time?"

❀ The next time came sooner than anyone expected. Chelm is a village, and the town square in any village is like a magnet. As the proverb goes, "If you wait in the town square, the world will come to you." Zalman Shelomo was walking though the town square on the way to the gate when he saw Gedaliah the Goniff coming toward him. "Good fortune smiles on me today," Zalman Shelomo thought to himself. "If he were walking away from me, I might never catch him." As it was, catch him he did, grabbing the goniff under his arm and swearing that this time he would not let go of him.

"Are you taking me directly to the mayor?" Gedaliah asked.

"Directly," answered Zalman Shelomo, "and afterward, the three of us will go directly to the rabbi. You will soon face justice and get what you justly deserve."

"The Town Hall is the other side of Chelm," said Gedaliah. "In the meantime, I have not eaten a bite today. It's already high noon. Have mercy, big fellow, and allow me to stop in Sissel's little café for a bite to eat. She'll feed us both and it will be my treat."

Zalman Shelomo hesitated for a moment, but the fact was that he had not obtained his wide stance by refusing to eat when the opportunity presented itself. Besides, Sissel was the best cook in town. Besides, he could sit at the table and never let Gedaliah out of his sight.

So they proceeded into the café, where they each had a meal of borscht and potatoes. As they finished eating, Gedaliah said, "Now, you just rest yourself here a moment while I pay for our food." And Zalman Shelomo rested for a minute.

He had not noticed it, but when the thief sat down at the table, he had taken a seat facing the door, which meant that Zalman Shelomo had automatically taken a seat across from him, a seat that faced the thief and not the door. When more than a few minutes had passed, Zalman Shelomo looked around. The thief was nowhere to be seen. He went to the little stand where Sissel sat near the door and asked, "Have you seen Gedaliah the Goniff?"

"He left a few minutes ago, saying you would pay the bill," answered Sissel.

Zalman Shelomo nodded sadly, and thought to himself, "Now my pocket, too, has been picked. But I will be wiser the next time."

❋ The next time came sooner than anyone could have expected. Zalman Shelomo saw Gedaliah sitting just off the town square, playing cards with three men. As stealthily as a large man could manage, he came up behind Gedaliah and grabbed his arm.

Gedaliah the Goniff laid down his hand and spoke to the men around the table, "I will be going now, but I thank you for the game. I have been taken prisoner by the industrious gatekeeper of Chelm."

"Now I have you well and truly," said Zalman Shelomo.

Gedaliah rose to his feet and said, "Well and truly, you have. Lead on, my good comrade."

The gatekeeper and the thief made an odd couple—the one thin as a pole, wiry and lithe; and the other a study in contrast.

"You cannot deceive me again," said Zalman Shelomo.

"I would not even try," said Gedaliah. "But I fear I will be sentenced to a long term in the prison."

"Very likely."

"And I have completely run out of snuff. I hardly think it would be civilized to force me to go that long time without snuff. And, behold, we are just passing the tobacconist's shop. Please, let us nip inside so that I can purchase a small tin of snuff."

"Better not. The last time you and I went into a shop together, you slipped out when I was not looking."

"I'll tell you what," Gedaliah said in a conspiratorial whisper, "this time you can stay right here while I go in. Then I will not be able to slip past you on the way out."

Zalman Shelomo thought this a wise plan. "Mind you," he told the thief, "it will go badly for you if you try to run."

"Farthest thing from my mind," answered Gedaliah. He went into the tobacco shop and Zalman waited. And waited.

And waited, until, at last, he went into the shop to see what had become of his prisoner, but Gedaliah was not in the shop. He turned to Baruch the Tobacconist and said, "What has become of that rascal, Gedaliah the Goniff?"

Baruch took a long draught of his pipe, blew an elegant smoke ring, and replied, "He left by the back door."

Zalman Shelomo nodded sadly and said to himself, "Now that thief has made me angry. I am wise to his tricks and he will not escape a third time."

❀ The third time was not a long time in coming. Zalman Shelomo, who was now prowling the streets from dawn to dusk, came upon Gedaliah the Goniff who was sunning himself on the benches beside the mikveh. Gedaliah's eyes were closed and his breathing was quiet. He might even have been sleeping.

Sleeping or not, Zalman Shelomo did not hesitate to arrange a rude awakening, grabbing the culprit under his arm and yanking him to his feet. "You will not escape me this time," he declared.

"Well, hello," said Gedaliah with a smile. "I did not expect you so soon again. I hope life is treating you well. How are your three little ones? And how is your winsome wife?"

"I am wise to your tricks," said Zalman Shelomo. "There's no time to discuss my sons and daughter or to tell you about my wife. There's only time to take you to the mayor and the rabbi, and that is what I am bound to do."

"I just thought that we were spending so much time in one another's company, we should be friendlier by now. Life is short and the finest enjoyment is a good friend."

"We can be friends after you are punished," the gatekeeper said, "but first you must be brought to justice. That is my job and I mean to do it."

They walked close together and Zalman Shelomo's hand never left Gedaliah's arm. His grip was firm and his intention was equally so.

"I have been lying in the sun for so long," Gedaliah began, "that I am parched with thirst. It's such a warm day under the summer sun. Surely, you must be thirsty, too."

"What of it?" asked Zalman Shelomo gruffly.

"In a moment, as you see, we will pass the tavern. What could be more natural for a couple of friends like us than that we imbibe a cup together?"

"What do you take me for?" asked Zalman Shelomo, growing edgy. "You escaped by slipping out the front door when you promised to pay at Sissel's café. You escaped by slipping out the back door when you promised to return to me at the tobacco shop. If I take you into the tavern, you will attempt to slip away again."

"Nevertheless, I know you are as thirsty as I am, friend. I will give you my word that I will not escape. I will not cheat by going out the front door, and I promise not to cheat by going out the back door."

"What do you propose?" asked Zalman Shelomo, who was both irritated and thirsty.

"The simplest of answers is nearly always the right one," said Gedaliah. "I will stand still, right here on this spot. You can go in to the tavern and get us both a drink. That way, I cannot escape."

Zalman Shelomo thought for a moment. Surely, Gedaliah was right. If he stood where he was, he could not go out either the front door or the back door. There was no way he could escape. So Zalman Shelomo let go of Gedaliah's arm, admonished him to remain precisely where he stood, and went into the tavern to buy drinks for the two of them.

He was gone only a moment or two, but when he returned the thief was gone. Zalman Shelomo paused long enough to drink both cups. This served to ease his frustration a bit.

He went home to his wife, the charming Gittele. He told her all that had happened with the thief and confessed that he was at his wit's end.

"The fault does not lie with you, my dear husband," Gittele said. "The fault lies with the other elders. By now, it is clear to you, and it must be clear to them that it would require three gatekeepers to capture this wily fellow: one to stand at the front door, one to stand at the back door, and one to stand beside him, holding him still. It's up to the elders to employ two more gatekeepers. Then you can undertake the arrest again."

"How wise you are, Gittele! I shall not chase this thief again until there are three of me."

From that day on, whenever Zalman Shelomo saw Gedaliah the Goniff, the two of them exchanged greetings, and Zalman Shelomo went on his way. And, truth be told, it made the citizens of Chelm swell with pride to know that their only professional thief was the wisest of all the goniffs.

WHAT BECAME OF THE OLD RABBI

❋ The shammes of Chelm had been called "Shammes" for so long that no one in Chelm remembered his given name. Some Chelmers were of the opinion that even the shammes did not remember it. His job was his life—to look after the synagogue and to be the rabbi's assistant. The shammes of Chelm had assisted the old rabbi, and now he assisted Reb Feivel.

Naturally, when one person occupies any position for a while, he comes to know "where the bodies are buried," as the saying goes. In the case of the shammes, this was true literally. The case in point is what happened to Isaac, the husband of Mirele the Nag.

As a rule, the women of Chelm are wise, so only a rare few manage to be less than kind to their husbands. True, it is written in the Scriptures that God created woman to be a "helpmate *against* her husband," which, as every yeshiva student knows, means that if a husband is good, his wife will stand with him as a support stands against a wall; but if a husband is bad, his wife will stand against him—either by torturing him or by enabling him to be even worse than he would be on his own.

Indubitably, Isaac was weak—too much of a gambler, too much of a lazybones, too much of a slacker. A wife like Mirele the Nag, however, was some justification for Isaac spending so much time in the synagogue, so much time at the tobacco shop, so much time at the gaming table—so much time, in short, away from home. For Mirele, nagging was a profession.

Her harangues began as whimpers, passed through whines, and elevated to squawks. She criticized everything Isaac did and did not do. Like an antique mirror, she distorted his every action into an affront.

Why had he not milked the goat? Did he think that the children would sit under it and suck the milk for themselves? Why had he not found a job? Did he think that she could run the household on water and turnips? Why had he tarried in the synagogue? Did he think the day should be spent entirely in asking God for forgiveness? Heaven knows, God might excuse him, but not she. She would never forgive him for marrying her when she had so many better offers. If only he had not hoodwinked her father, today she would be married to the rich Reb Fishel or to the butcher. She would be a lady of means, or at least she would be eating meat instead of borscht.... And when was he planning to milk the goat?

So it went, without end, until one spring day Isaac, husband of Mirele the Nag, disappeared. At first, Mirele took little notice. "Good riddance," she commented at the river where the women came to do laundry. "Hardly a thing has been lost!" But a week went by and Mirele had no one to berate.

Now that she missed her beloved Isaac, she nagged everyone who was anyone, "Where is he? Is he hiding at your house? Have you seen him anywhere? Why aren't you out searching? Maybe he was trapped by a bear in the forest. He could be sitting in a tree waiting for help. God knows, his voice does not carry. Such a good man," she remembered fondly. "He never raised his voice to me. In fact, he would not dare. Maybe he is afraid to raise his voice now even if he is in trouble. Help me, have pity on me."

The elders of Chelm took up the issue. This disruption had to end. Mirele the Nag was driving the whole town crazy. It went unsaid, but all believed Isaac had left of his own volition. Yet, none of them was brave enough to broach this possibility to Mirele. In the end—after sending out for food four times—they decided to send out search parties to look for Isaac.

The first set of four men went up the mountain, even crossing over to the other side, but returned to report that they had found no trace of Isaac. Another search party of four rowed up and down the river talking to fishermen, but none of the fishermen recalled any stranger passing them. The third search party went as far as Lvov and found no trace of Isaac on the way there or back. Only one direction was left, so the last search party went into the forest.

They came back like the scouts of Moses returning from the Holy Land. Stretched across the shoulders of the four was a long, sturdy tree branch. Dangling from the middle of the branch, just like the huge bunch of grapes in the Bible, was a body. As they came through the gate of Chelm, Zalman Shelomo the Gatekeeper ran (as best he was able to run in consideration of the weight he carried) to alert the elders. By the time the four scouts with their burden reached the town square, the elders were assembled on the steps of the Town Hall.

As you might imagine, news in Chelm spreads like water in a sponge. The Chelmers assembled almost as quickly as the elders. Zelig the Bedecked, mayor of Chelm, stared down at the body and loudly declared, "We have found the missing Isaac! May his memory be for a blessing."

"Not so fast," Tzeitel the Butcher's Wife said. "Before you declare that this is Isaac, someone should identify him."

Like a barbershop quartet, the four searchers sang out in unison, "That may not be so easy."

Bending over the body, Raisel the Matchmaker, who had made the match (or mismatch) between Isaac and Mirele the Nag, and who therefore thought she would surely recognize Isaac, said, "Mayor, I think there is something here you should see."

The mayor bent closer to the body and the elders did the same. The closer they came, the more it seemed as if a spell had been cast over them. One by one, they straightened up and stood speechless. Finally, Naftali the Water Carrier managed a choked voice to announce, "This body has no head."

"The work of a witch?" Sissel wondered aloud. And, at this juncture, most of the women of Chelm spit two times and ejaculated the words, "Pooh! Pooh!" (This was meant to clear the air so that the work of any witch would not affect them or their households.)

"More likely, the work of a bear who bit the head clean off," Naftali surmised. Secretly, however, it passed his mind that Mirele the Nag might have been the one who bit off her husband's head.

"Oy!" the mayor intoned. "If only the rabbi could offer an answer. This is definitely the kind of concern a rabbi should handle." The mayor's eyes focused on the shammes with a significant stare.

"Impossible," said the shammes. "You know it is impossible."

Hirschel the Wood Carrier suggested, "Let us begin at the beginning. Can Mirele say if this is the body of her Isaac?"

Mirele the Nag had been close by all this time. She came forward, dropped to her knees, and inspected the body shoulder to toes. She felt the arms and the legs. She looked into the empty pockets of the jacket. Then she lifted her hands to her face and said, "For the life of me, I do not know if this is my Isaac or not."

Raisel suggested, "Perhaps we should undress him?"

Mirele grimaced. "It wouldn't help."

Sissel said, "Mirele, think back: The last time you saw Isaac, did he have a head?"

"That's just it," said Mirele. "I remember yelling at him and telling him he was a rapscallion, but I paid no attention at all to his head. He was out and about and away from home so much that I can hardly remember his face. What if, all along, he didn't have a head?"

Baruch the Tobacconist chimed in, "It was like that when Isaac played cards. He always covered his face with the cards he was playing. Frankly, he might just have been holding the cards above his neck. I can't swear that he had a head!"

"And the last time I scolded him," Mirele said thoughtfully, the hint of a teardrop in her eye, "he put his hands above his neck—though I thought he was covering his face—and he ran through the house crying, 'I must be losing my head. I must be losing my head.' I guess he did."

Then she added, "But I swear I have not seen his head since he disappeared, and I have cleaned the house twice."

Then she added, "And if one of the children had found his head, they surely would have let me know."

"Vey!" said the mayor. "It's no simple matter. Perhaps Isaac had a head; perhaps he did not. We need the rabbi's judgment. Perhaps a case like this happened before. The rabbi would know if such a thing is recorded in the Holy Books. We must ask the rabbi."

He turned to the shammes. "*You* must ask the rabbi."

"It will do no good," the shammes replied.

"You must try," the mayor said.

So the shammes set out on what he knew was a wild goose chase. "It will do no good," he mumbled to himself. Truth be told, he was more correct than he could ever have imagined. Truth be told, it was more of a wild goose chase than he could ever have foreseen. To comprehend what is about to ensue, you will need a few facts.

✹ Two years before, the rabbi, now referred to as "the old rabbi of Chelm," built a *sukkah*, a "booth," the traditional three-sided shack used to celebrate the holiday of *Sukkot* or "Booths." During the days of this holy season, Jews eat meals in the sukkah and some even sleep in the sukkah to remind them of how much trust their ancient semi-nomadic ancestors placed in God alone. Unlike their semi-nomadic ances-

tors, however, inclement weather—high winds, rain, hail, or
snow—would send the Chelmers back into the comforts of
their homes. Normally, that is. But the old rabbi of Chelm,
Rebbe Pinchas, was made of stern stuff. He went into the
sukkah on the first evening of Sukkot that year, sat down beside the table, put on his *tallis* (his well-worn prayer shawl);
and never again came out.

When the winter rains arrived that year, the shammes
begged Rebbe Pinchas to come indoors where it was warm
and dry. Rebbe Pinchas answered only with silence. He did
not budge from the table. So the shammes fetched a ladder
and replaced the leafy twigs and branches that usually comprise the ceiling of a sukkah with pine boards. Still the rain
found its way into the sukkah since the fourth side was wide
open. The shammes brought more boards, piling them up beside the sukkah, intending to wall up the fourth side and
make a door. But the rains were so fierce just then that he
had to postpone his work for a day or two.

Lo, when the rains finally let up and the shammes returned, he discovered that the rabbi had done the job for him.
The sukkah now had four sides and a roof. No door. Instead of
a door, Rebbe Pinchas had cut out a small opening at the bottom of the fourth wall, a passage through which only a skinny
person or a child could go.

The shammes was the rabbi's assistant. He remained
calm and polite. He knocked on the new wall. When there
was no response from within, he cleared his throat and
called, "Rebbe Pinchas, are you in there?" Still no response.
So the shammes went down on all fours and stared into the
small opening. As soon as his eyes adjusted to the darkness,
he saw the reassuring outline of the rabbi's legs.

Thereafter, he brought meals to Rebbe Pinchas three
times a day, passing them through the hole. The rabbi sometimes ate and sometimes did not eat. From time to time, the
shammes crouched by the opening to listen, or to ask, "Rebbe
Pinchas, do you need anything?" Once, he thought he heard

the rabbi mumbling the blessings after eating. That was all. Until one day, collecting the food tray, he found a note from the rabbi. The note read: "No more QUESTIONS!"

The elders of Chelm called an emergency meeting. They read the note over and over. They conferred for seven days and seven nights discussing, debating, deliberating.

Raisel the Matchmaker was deeply concerned: "A rabbi without a wife is good for business. A rabbi who sits alone in a sukkah is a hard sell. On the other hand, a man who will not talk back… it's just possible that he might be merchandised."

Yankel the Tailor was bemused. "If this solitary existence becomes a trend, no one will need new clothes, and old clothes will not need mending."

The three sages offered three opinions. The first said, "Rebbe Pinchas was always a quiet man." The second said, "Wise rabbis know it is always best to be silent." The third said, "Plainly, Rebbe Pinchas has just run out of ANSWERS!"

The elders finally resolved to table the issue of the rabbi in the sukkah, so that now, two years later, as the shammes approached the sukkah to ask the rabbi a question, he could only mutter to himself, "I will ask, but it will do no good."

And he would have asked. He started to ask. Then he thought, "Perhaps I will get down by the opening and ask from there." So he dropped to his hands and knees and put his face to the dark booth. His eyes soon adjusted to the darkness and he saw nothing. Nothing but the table and chair. He cried out, "Rebbe Pinchas," but to no avail. Anxiously, he squeezed himself through the hole and stood. No Rebbe Pinchas. Nothing but the table and chair.

The shammes was a wise man of Chelm, so he pondered the problem. Perhaps the rabbi had eaten so little that he had shrunk down to nothing. If so, his soul might still be in the sukkah. Perhaps the shammes should put the question to the soul of the rabbi. Yet, if the rabbi himself had been silent, imagine how silent the soul of the rabbi would be. Still, it would not hurt to try. Perhaps the rabbi had been silent, but his soul was longing to be loquacious—in the same way, the shammes reasoned, that he himself was poor, but his soul longed to be rich.

So it happened that the shammes stood in the empty sukkah, telling Rebbe Pinchas' soul the story of Isaac and Mirele the Nag and how the search parties had scouted the land, and how the headless body had been found, and how the mayor insisted that only a case from the Holy Books could solve this heady problem. And he told it all without asking a single question since the rabbi's instructions were, "No more QUESTIONS!"

If the soul of Rebbe Pinchas were there, it did not respond.

Shaking his head, the shammes went back to report to the mayor and the elders, all still standing around the body. He was brief, but succinct. "Rebbe Pinchas has turned up missing."

"Ha!" Tzeitel cried, pointing a finger at the mayor. "Now you see that rushing to call this body Isaac is entirely foolish. It may just as easily be the body of Rebbe Pinchas."

There was a lot of spitting twice and "Pooh! Pooh!"-ing. And Avrom the Barrel Maker, standing in the crowd, put his head down, saying, "Heaven protect us."

Zelig the Bedecked said, "But we do not know that the rabbi is dead."

Hirschel the Wood Carrier said, "And we do not know that Isaac is dead. But surely this headless body must belong to one of them."

Tzeitel the Butcher's Wife grabbed hold of the shammes by his jacket. "Tell me, and think carefully before you tell me: The last time you saw Rebbe Pinchas, did he have a head?"

The shammes pulled away. He calmed himself before answering. "For a long time now, all I could see of the rabbi were his legs."

"And before that?" demanded Sissel. "Did he have a head before he walled himself into the sukkah?"

"You are all witnesses," replied the shammes. "It was always Rebbe Pinchas' custom to wear his tallis over his head."

The mayor was beside himself. "There is never a rabbi around when you need one," he complained to no one in particular.

Mirele the Nag was beside herself, "Even in death, my Isaac finds a way to vex me!"

Raisel the Matchmaker added, "Before this, it was just possible I might have found him a good wife, but now...."

Then she added, "On the other hand, if a woman has a good enough head on her shoulders, it might suffice for her and her husband, too. It's often the case."

The body was turned over to Chelm's burial society and prepared for burial in a pine box made from the boards of the sukkah. This was a nice touch since the elders felt that if the body truly belonged to the old rabbi, he would at least be comforted by remaining in his sukkah for eternity. And, alternatively, if the body belonged to Isaac, he would be comforted by spending the time waiting for the World to Come away from his home and in the blessed silence of the old rabbi's sukkah.

Two funerals were held for the body, one right after another. The old rabbi's funeral came first, for as one sage averred, "Some honor should be paid to a rabbi, even one who no longer has the ANSWERS." The mayor spoke for the rabbi. He rose to the occasion with some deathless words:

"How appropriate that Holy Scriptures have a parallel to offer Rebbe Pinchas. Is it not true that King Ahasuerus once put the question to Haman—may his name be cursed—'What shall be done for the one whom the king wishes to honor?' And is it not also true that it was the selfsame Haman—may his name be cursed—the King beheaded! Can we say less of Rebbe Pinchas? God, our immortal King, works in mysterious ways to honor His servants. If He wishes to behead one, who is to say that it is not for a blessing?"

The people of Chelm responded, "Amen."

With that, the second funeral began, in honor of Isaac. His wife, Mirele the Nag, spoke. She began in a kind of whine and built to a crescendo.

"Who can accuse you of deserting me, my little turnip? As you go to the grave, you will not be any lazier than you were before you lost your head. No, and you will not provide any better than you once did. And who will milk the goat now that you are gone? Do you imagine that I have twenty hands? That I could embrace the children and do the housework and also milk the goat? What kind of man are you, now that you are dead? Useless, like you were when you were alive!" She ran out of breath just then, gave a deep moan, and concluded, "We shall miss you, the children and me."

The people of Chelm whispered, "Amen." It was the first word they could get in edgewise.

Two graves were dug. In even years, the coffin lies buried in the grave marked "PINCHAS OF OZCOPY, REBBE OF CHELM." In odd years, the shammes moves the body to the grave marked by the words of his beloved Mirele: "ISAAC OF CHELM. HUSBAND, FATHER, SHIRKER."

When the new rabbi, Reb Feivel, came to Chelm, the shammes was pleased to assist him. Not long after, when they were alone together in the synagogue, Reb Feivel turned to the shammes and said, "Between us, I have to ask: What became of the old rabbi of Chelm?"

The shammes merely shrugged his shoulders and said, "The old rabbi ran out of ANSWERS."

THE FISH STORY

❀ The fishermen of Chelm brought in fresh fish from the river but not always the fish that the Chelmers wanted. There was a definite craving among the wise men and women for the tangy, salty taste of herring. Herring in vinegar. Herring pickled. Herring in wine. Herring in sour cream. Smoked herring. The craving was greatest when the onions were harvested in late summer and early fall. But there was no herring in the river. So some fishermen temporarily became bargemen, making the long river journey to Brisk where they traded Chelm's hemp, tobacco, and lumber for barrels of salted and pickled herring that had made the long journey from the Baltic Sea.

The fishermen of Chelm chatted as the barge floated back toward Chelm. Like wise men everywhere, they saw the difficulties of their work and wondered if it might not be simplified. All this salting, pickling, and packing in barrels. All this shipping, trading, and shipping again. All to get barrels of herring to Chelm. There ought to be a more convenient solution!

"Fish are smart," said Dovidl the Nose. (His nickname could have been born of his accurate sense of where the fish were and the nets should be thrown. Or, as many townsfolk thought, it might have originated based on the rich aroma sensed whenever he came nigh.) "How many times have I almost caught Grandfather Pike, only to see him slip out of my net?"

"He is surely the largest fish I have ever seen," observed Moishe the Elder. (His epithet, "the Elder," was entirely explicable. It derived from his wife Tzippie giving him only sons. At birth, the first was called Moishe the Younger—thereby achieving for Moishe, the father, the addition of "the Elder." When Tzippie brought forth a second son, the baby was aptly named Moishe the Younger and the former Moishe the Younger was renamed Moishe the Middle. This arrangement was not to last, for a third son came along the next year. To avoid confusion and keep from renaming everyone each time a new boy appeared, the baby was called Moishe the Youngest. The fourth son posed a greater problem. Tzippie suggested a number of alternatives: "Moishe the Younger Yet," "Moishe the Very Youngest," and "Moishe Most Current." Moishe the Elder suggested "Moishele," and that name stuck. Another issue arose, however. Their eldest son, Moishe the Middle, was no longer the middle. This resolved itself as his personality suggested that his nickname be suitably transformed to Moishe the Meddler—and so he is known today.)

"I know where that mammoth fish lives—on the far side of the river from Chelm," said Dovidl the Nose, "but it does me no good to know. Why, Grandfather Pike is almost a Chelmer himself, wise enough to evade us time and time again."

The other fishermen nodded. Motke Mendel lit up his pipe and sat back. In a matter-of-fact way, he said, "My papa told me the story of Grandfather Pike's greatest escape."

"Ho, that's a tale every Chelmer should know!" said Dovidl the Nose. "I know it, of course, but go on and tell it the way your papa told it to you—for the sake of Havel. He's the youngest among us." Actually, they were all happy to hear a story.

Havel, only fourteen, was now officially a fisherman. From the age of eight, he used to hang out where fishermen and their wives repaired the nets along the shore beside the dock. His father, Shmul the Fishmonger, had a little shop on the town square. But Havel yearned to be in the boats, on the open water, and away from the store. So, he delightedly stretched out his lanky adolescent frame against one of the barrels and waited for the story.

Just so, everyone on board adjusted themselves in comfortable positions. Moishe the Elder took a pinch of snuff, resulting in a few sniffles and a sneeze. At the tiller, Dovidl raised a jug of schnapps, took a drink, and passed it to Havel, who drank and coughed. Motke Mendel's pipe sent a trail of blue-white smoke billowing off to trail the barge. He began his tale:

"Papa remembered when Grandfather Pike was younger and stronger, already the largest fish on the river, but not as crafty as he is now. It was springtime, just before Passover, and the trout were running upstream. That year, they were leaping in the river, fairly flying, and the men could hardly get their nets out fast enough to harvest them. No one was thinking pike, so that is when it happened. A heavy net came up with a handful of trout and the biggest pike ever!

"When they emptied the net on the deck, the pike seemed about to flip and flop his way out of the boat. It took two fishermen, some say three, to corral him and stand in his way. Somebody said, 'Clobber him, kill him,' but the captain shouted, 'What? Are you crazy? The money that fish will fetch if we only bring it in alive and fresh! Let some rich woman's maid kill it in her kitchen.' So every effort was turned to keeping that pike alive.

"First, they dipped a pail in the river and brought it up full of river water. Then, they put the fish in the pail. At any moment, parts of the pike were in the pail and parts were out. That pail was no fit. The pike's tail was flapping over one side and the head refused the pail entirely. Never ceasing its movement, the pike slapped most of the water from the pail.

"Next, the captain suggested the barrel of fresh water on the boat. A desperate enterprise! If the fishermen weren't only a short distance from the dock, they could threaten their own lives by depriving themselves of fresh water. But the trout had been so plentiful that they had not gone far from Chelm. So they dumped out the drinking water and formed a chain to dip pails and pass them until the barrel was fairly full of river water. They threw in the handful of trout—for, so they reasoned, they might as well keep them fresh, too. Then they approached the pike, still wriggling and thumping the deck with its tail.

"'Okay, boys, lift him,' said the captain. But before they could lift the pike, they had to grab him. One sailor took hold of a fin so slippery it passed right through his fist. Another sailor was thrown halfway across the deck when the pike's tail caught him just so. Then the captain shouted, 'Herring!'

"'Here goes lunch,' said one of the fisherman as he threw a piece of herring in front of the big pike. And it worked. The pike wriggled and half-swam to the herring, gulping it down. One piece of herring after another, until the pike had maneuvered itself to the other end of the deck and was right by the barrel. 'Now, grab him,' yelled the captain, and three fishermen lunged for the pike. One was struck by the tail and fell overboard. The other two managed to grab the pike near the head and under the belly. 'Lift,' the captain shouted, and the two lifted the pike into the air, even as the pike was still wriggling and its tail was still wildly thrashing. It was nip and tuck, tuck and nip. Would the pike fall into the barrel or would it manage to flip over the top of the barrel and into the river? The captain saw the danger and he himself ran to aid the two struggling fishermen.

"He should have walked, not run. The captain slipped. His legs flew out from under him. He fell flat on his backside. Pain coursed through him, but he yelled to the two fishermen, 'Don't lose him, boys, I'll be up in a minute to help you.' He stood and discovered that one of his ankles was twisted. 'A curse on you,' he yelled, pointing at the pike as he painfully hobbled toward the two fishermen.

"The boat swayed just then; the fishermen lost their grip on the pike and it fell back to the ship's deck, twisting this way and that, using its tail to get out of the captain's way as he fell again with a second dreadful cry of distress. He knew at once that he had broken his wrist. The two fishermen tried to help him up, but the captain fairly screamed at them, 'Forget me! Get that pike into the barrel!' Also, he was heard to murmur, 'Double the pain, but never mind. I shall double the price.'

"The fishermen made for the pike again, but the pike now made for the captain. The big fish was upon the fallen sailor in an instant and his powerful tail slapped the captain full in the face. 'Ho, that eye will be black in the morning,' one fisherman said. Another, knowing the captain's temper, glanced at his mate and made a sign with his finger for him to be silent.

"'Get me up!' the captain bellowed. 'I will have vengeance on that pike!' They lifted the captain to the bench. One fisherman brought him a club, saying, 'Strike that villain and be done with it!' But the captain pushed the club away. 'Not for this fish,' he said. 'It is not enough! Justice must be done to this fish!'

"And that is what was done. The captain served as the judge and three fishermen were the jury. A fourth fisherman poured pails full of river water over the pike to keep him alive during the trial. For the many insults to the captain—for the injuries to the captain's bottom, his leg, his arm, and his dignity—the pike was sentenced to death—the worst death any fisherman could imagine—death by drowning. 'Let him walk the plank!' the captain ordered. They put a bench halfway over the side (it was the closest thing to a plank they could manage), hoisted the pike on to the bench, and coaxed it to walk by throwing bits of herring in its path. Five minutes later, it was over. The great pike fell from the far edge of the bench into the river to drown."

Motke Mendel paused long enough to tamp his pipe against the side of the barge. "My father told me that Grandfather Pike swam away without looking back. And the captain—a man of reasonable wit, a Chelmer, and therefore a man of wisdom—realized that justice would be delayed that day. 'That's one damned stubborn fish,' he spat out. 'Not only does he refuse to be put in a barrel, he even refuses to drown!'"

THE WINTER OF DISCONTENT

❀ Reb Fishel and his wife, Minda Leah, lived in a house overlooking the village of Chelm. The cobbler, the tailor, the butcher, and others looked forward to days when Reb Fishel or Minda Leah shopped. Not that they were the only wealthy family in Chelm. Half a dozen other houses occupied the same shoulder of the mountain, creating Chelm's wealthy neighborhood.

Reb Fishel's prosperity derived from his lumber mill which manufactured finished pinewood beams, planks, slats, and boards. His lumber was shipped by ox cart and barge to cities where people could afford to build with finished wood. In Chelm, building was done the old-fashioned way. Chelmers brought down trees, trimmed branches, split logs, cut mortise and tenon joints, and hammered. They often reused planks and boards from older or abandoned houses and barns. The ramshackle houses of Chelm stood testament to the home-made, the rough-hewn.

Not that the poor did not wish to be wealthy. But how was a simple goatherd expected to make more than a living when he slaved night and day just to feed his family? How was the cobbler, despite an occasional order from Minda Leah or Reb Fishel, supposed to get rich when he could hardly afford to shoe the twelve feet of his family? The dairyman had milk for his household, but never cream; and most folk in Chelm milked their goats, reserving the more expensive cow's milk to make cheese (though they often made do

49

with goat cheese). The finest leather was earmarked for The Hill, the enclave of rich Chelmers who lived up above. The best fish from Shmul's fish shop never graced the mouths of his wife or children; even the butcher, who supplied meat for Tzeitel and his three little ones, reserved the best cuts for The Hill.

In the synagogue, rich Chelmers claimed the best seats, those along the eastern wall, close beside the Holy Ark. In town meetings, they sat at the front, mingling with the elders. When the wealthy walked through the town square, they expected average Chelmers to step aside and make way for them. They traveled in covered buggies; they wore fur coats and fur hats in the winter. They dressed in satin and wool. They expected respect.

Of course, when people are poor and their neighbors are poor, then being poor seems natural. As the Chelmers told one another, "It's no disgrace to be poor—which is the only good thing you can say about it." Poor children enjoyed childhood without expensive toys and dolls. Poor families shared what they had with one another, with neighbors, with friends. Borscht tastes sweet to the poor; beer can be as tasty as plum schnapps.

So what caused the vile attack of disaffection in Chelm? It was the winter of rain, hail, and snow.

Rain came first, soaking the village for a week, translating streets and paths into sentences of mud punctuated with puddle periods. Walking was torturous for adults and hazardous for small children. The Hill went untroubled by the rains. They expected Hirschel the Wood Carrier to bring them wood for their fireplaces and Naftali the Water Carrier to bring them water. They sent maids to town to shop for food for their tables. They stayed indoors. They were not drenched, nor were they forced to contend with the mud.

When the streets were mud, and the ruts in the streets were rivulets, hail fell. It was not so constant as the rain, but, intermittently for days, it fell in the size of acorns and hard enough to bruise. Off and on, it came down the size of plums. The mud turned to slush and iced over; streets were ever more treacherous. Weak roofs were pummeled and pierced. Chelmers were afraid, venturing out only when it was urgent to do so. Often enough, of course: When you have to go, you have to go. Enough said.

The snow followed, falling gently, at first, but steadily for days. Oh, the Chelmers tried to comfort one another, passing the time by telling snow stories, including some rather old chestnuts.

One January, according to one story, so much snow fell in Chelm that the townsfolk complained to the elders. The elders met for seven days and seven nights, debating ways to rid Chelm of snow. At last, relying as politicians will do, on the law, they passed a resolution banning all snow from Chelm. To enforce the ban, they organized "snow brigades." Men, women, and children were armed with shovels and pails. From the town center, snow was put in pails and pails were passed hand-to-hand to the last person in each brigade who stood on a ladder and tossed the snow over the wall and out of Chelm. The work went on continuously, until, by the month of May, Chelm was snow-free.

One March, another story told, the snowfall created a breathtakingly beautiful scene. No one in Chelm was crass enough to disturb such natural elegance. Families stared from their doorways and gazed from their windows, absorbed by the wonder of God's world in bridal white. Zalman Shelomo, a sensitive man despite his girth, complained to the elders. "How shall I open the gates of Chelm if I cannot walk to them? And how can I walk to them without leaving a trail of ugly footsteps in the road?" The elders debated. At last, they decided. Zalman Shelomo was forced to sit on a table while four men carried the table to the gate. So it was, the story concludes, that not one of Zalman Shelomo's footfalls disturbed the glistening snow.

But these stories were scant comfort while, in fact, the snow changed from its first placid downfall to a raging blizzard. Chelmers could hardly move outdoors—they could barely stand against the winds, much less walk against them. Shops were closed. Sheep and goats were herded into their owners' houses where they bumped into tables and chairs, stepped on children, and fed on straw beds. Horses and cows, too far out to be reached, froze where they pastured. Stables were full, cowsheds overcrowded, and chicken coops too flimsy to protect the unfortunate fowl closest to the walls.

When the snow ended, Chelmers emerged to inspect the damage. They were demoralized. For an already impoverished population, the destruction and loss were unbearable. As if to place a point upon their plight, one day later the roof of the Town Hall, over-weighted by snow, collapsed.

The elders met in an emergency session. The synagogue was filled from wall to wall with Chelmers. Even the half who seldom came to synagogue to pray, came today in despair. As soon as Zelig the Bedecked, mayor of Chelm, announced that the meeting was open, complaint followed complaint.

"How can I push my cart in streets that are nothing but mud? How?"

"How will I feed my children when I have not been able to work for weeks? How?"

"My bed was eaten by my goat. How will I afford another? How?"

"That's nothing. Who will replace my frozen ox? How will I plow without my ox? How?"

"We were already poor, now we are poorer yet."

"We were already suffering, now suffering would be a relief."

Until someone cried, "We are suffering, but *they* are not."

"*They?*"

"The rich! The Hill! We are suffering, but *they* are not."

"Rabbi, explain it to us," pled Anshel the Tailor's Son. "Why do the rich prosper and the poor suffer? Why do the rich dress in fine clothes while we dress in rags? Why do the rich eat the choicest cuts of meat while we eat fish and turnips? Why do the rich deserve to sit near the Holy Ark in the synagogue while we are forced to sit far from it? Why do the rich live on cream while we are forced to live on air? Why is there no justice in Chelm?"

Reb Fishel and Minda Leah—along with others from The Hill—were sitting close together, as they always did. Now, angry eyes turned toward them. Minda Leah rose to her feet and said, "We are ready to do our share to help." From his seat, Reb Fishel made clear his intent: "We will make loans."

"Again with the loans?" groaned one of the farmers. "What use are the loans if we cannot afford to repay them?"

Minda Leah sensed the climate. She scrutinized her neighbors from The Hill, cast a steady gaze on her husband, and announced, "We'll make some gifts."

"Gifts?" cried Kalman the Fixer. "You know what the Holy Books say: 'Gifts make slaves like yokes make oxen.' We don't want gifts. We want justice."

Minda Leah sat down. What could she say?

Reb Feivel, the Glory of Chelm, stood. "The poor want justice and cannot find it in Chelm. Yet our Holy Books speak of justice, so there must be justice in the world, even if there is no justice in Chelm."

Reb Fishel stood, "If there is justice in the world, I am willing to buy some for Chelm."

A murmur of suspicion passed through the throng, but the poor soon realized they were receiving their best offer. So they applauded.

Reb Feivel was relieved and gladly resumed his seat. He fell asleep and snored as the discussion continued.

"Surely, there is justice in Lvov," said Avrom the Barrel Maker. "I have seen Lvov and there is nothing like The Hill there. Rich and poor in Lvov live on the same level."

Shmul the Fishmonger urged, "Let us send two men to Lvov to buy justice for Chelm."

It was put to a vote and agreed. Reb Fishel gave a purse full of twenty gold coins to Zev the Treasurer as he had promised. All that was left was for the elders of Chelm to work out the details of the Justice-Purchasing Program. One concern after another was raised and met.

Would justice be light or heavy? If light, women could be sent to fetch it. If heavy, best to send men. The outcome? Best to send men, just in case it was heavy.

Would justice be big or little? If little, a couple of men might be able to transport it by hand. If big, would an ox cart suffice? This debate ended with practical concerns about the road. An ox cart was likely to get stuck repeatedly in the mud and snow. Best to send a donkey cart.

Who would go? The men should be hardy, but they should not be the only support of their families. They should be men who could guard the money on the way to Lvov and the justice on the way home. They should be models of wisdom—men who would recognize justice when they saw it. They should not be so heavy that they themselves would weigh down the donkey cart.

Anshel the Tailor's Son was chosen for his youth, strength, and wisdom—it was also a plus that he was thin as a poplar sprout. Ansel the Tinsmith was chosen for wisdom, for age (he was nearly fifty-five), and for being a bachelor. "Besides," observed Raisel the Matchmaker, "an Ansel and an Anshel—a fine-sounding match." The meeting ended; the Chelmers dispersed.

✸ Ansel and Anshel rode the donkey cart to Lvov. Ansel said, "No doubt, the place to find justice is the courthouse." They went and stood by the courthouse. Anshel asked people going in, "Do you know where we might find justice?" Ansel asked people coming out. Every answer was much the same: "If there is justice here in Lvov, you will find none here."

Imagine their surprise when two fellows from Lvov approached them. "We hear you are from Chelm. Is that true?" the tall one asked.

"Most assuredly," said Ansel.

"And we hear you are looking to find justice. Is that true?" the short one asked.

"Absolutely," said Anshel. "You see that donkey and cart? We have brought it so we can carry some justice back to Chelm."

"In that case," said the tall one, "you will please come with us. We have a whole warehouse full of justice only a short distance from here."

As they walked, the short one said, "The fact is, we have more justice than we can use. These days, people are more often seeking advantage instead of justice, so we're loaded with justice and we can make you a good bargain."

When they reached the warehouse, the two men opened the door. Anshel and Ansel could scarce believe their eyes! Before them, stacked from wall to wall and from floor to ceiling, was barrel upon barrel.

"How much justice can you afford?" the tall man inquired.

Anshel and Ansel asked for a moment to confer. The two men from Lvov politely withdrew. The Chelmers began to debate the subject in whispers, but just as the debate was progressing, the tall man returned and said, "Excuse me, I thought you should know; we only sell justice by the barrel. Do you think you can afford a whole barrel?"

Anshel decided to be clever. After all, the coins in the purse belonged to the people of Chelm. He knew he had twenty gold pieces, so he said, "We have ten gold coins."

The tall man and his companion whispered to one another. So Anshel had second thoughts. "We might have fifteen gold coins," he told them, "if we could get a whole barrel of justice."

"That might help," said the tall one, and he returned to whispering with his companion.

Ansel now broke his silence. "We have twenty gold coins and not a farthing more."

The men from Lvov turned to the men from Chelm. The short one clapped Ansel on the back. "Stout fellow," he said, "not to worry. Do we look like cads? We would never take your last coin. We can let you have a barrel full of justice for only nineteen gold coins."

Hands were shaken and the deal was struck. The barrel turned out to be lighter than it looked and the donkey had little trouble on the way back to Chelm.

❀ As the trio—Ansel, Anshel, and the donkey—approached Chelm, the townsfolk gathered. Justice was arriving! Rich and poor alike were anxious to receive it.

In front of the synagogue, the barrel was lowered from the wagon and set on the ground. Zelig the Bedecked, mayor of Chelm, called on Avrom the Barrel Maker to pry off the lid. But as soon as the barrel was open, the aroma of decaying fish pervaded the air.

Jumping away from the barrel, Avrom exclaimed, "This justice is spoiled!"

"Alas, the justice is rotten!" declared Tzeitel.

Only the rich Reb Fishel was not surprised. "It confirms my belief," he stated authoritatively. "Spoiled justice is the only kind you will ever find outside of Chelm."

Reb Feivel, the Glory of Chelm, sneezed. He had taken quite a jolt by breathing in the stench from the barrel. Now, he raised his hands in the air. "Please, please," he began, "I think I understand. The problem here is not rotten justice. The problem here is the wisdom of Chelm."

There was silence as the rabbi explained, "We have always known that Chelmers are wise—why, any child in Chelm is wiser than the sagest sage beyond Chelm's wall—and this is the proof. Out of Chelm, this," he raised his forefinger high in the air, then dropped it to point to the offending barrel, "this is what passes for justice. We are wise enough to know just by the odor their justice is spoiled, but to the benighted souls who live in Lvov, justice smells as sweet to them as plum pudding. Since we Chelmers are wiser, we must devise our own justice.

"Here is what I propose: From now on, whenever animals are butchered, let every cut of meat be the choicest cut. From now on, let there be no difference between sackcloth and lace, silk and cotton. From now on, let every synagogue wall be the eastern wall and let every seat be equally near the Holy Ark.

"One thing more: If the rich are foolish enough to pay a premium for seats that were formerly close to the Holy Ark, let them. If the rich insist on paying more for what used to be the finest silk, let them. If they persist in paying more for cuts of meat that were formerly choicer, let them. Wisdom is what sets apart a true Chelmer!"

To this day, no one knows whether the crowd was more stirred by the rabbi's proposal or by the rabbi's devastating logic, but the effect was thrilling! They applauded, and many emitted an "Amen!" aloud, as if the rabbi had delivered a sermon.

Zelig the Bedecked, the mayor of Chelm, swelled with pride. "No wonder we call Reb Feivel, 'the Glory of Chelm!' His wisdom speaks for itself." A vote was taken then and there and the people of Chelm—townsfolk and Hill folk—accepted the rabbi's proposal unanimously.

Forbearance returned to Chelm after that. Spring was in the air. The streets dried (as much as they ever dried) and the mud abated (as much as it ever abated). The rich still lived on The Hill and pretended nothing had changed, but the poor knew better. They might still be poor, but now they knew they were equal to the rich. They ate the choicest meat, wore the finest clothes, and sat in the best seats in the synagogue—no matter what they ate, no matter what they wore, no matter where they sat.

As for Reb Feivel, everyone agreed, "The new rabbi fits us like a fine slipper; he is as wise as the wisest Chelmer."

TOWN HALL

✿ It was time to rebuild Town Hall. The elders wanted the new one to be grander and more impressive than the old hall. Zev the Treasurer, however, pointedly reminded them that the town treasury was neither grander nor more impressive than it had ever been.

"We can still use the foundation of the old Town Hall," said Kalman the Fixer, a man who never threw anything away. "The locks and the keys are still good and so is the prison fence."

Hirschel the Wood Carrier asked, "How do we remove the old building?"

Sissel the Tzimmes Maker made the first suggestion: "Why not push the old Town Hall off the foundation? I heard a house was once moved all the way across Chelm just by pushing."

"You heard a fable," said Zalman Shelomo the Gate-keeper. "My uncle was there when it happened. That house was plagued. It had been built too close to the mountain; every year the spring runoff flooded it. The elders decided the house should be moved away from the mountain, and a dozen Chelmers came out early one summer morning to move it. They pushed for two hours without budging it, so they recruited a dozen more Chelmers. By that time the sun was high in the sky. The men took off their jackets and threw them all in a pile. Then they set their shoulders against the house and shoved, and rammed, and thrust.

"After a few hours, one of the men looked up and said, 'We have pushed far enough!' The others asked, 'How do you know?' 'Look,' he said, 'we have gone so far we can no longer see the pile of jackets.' And that was certainly true. So everyone, including my uncle, stopped pushing.

"It was a huge mystery. They had evidently moved the house so far that not only could they not see their jackets, they could no longer find the place where the pile of jackets had been. But Gedaliah the Goniff—accursed thief that he is!—solved the mystery all by himself. He offered to sell my uncle back his jacket. Every one of the men bought back his own jacket that day. And they all learned a lesson: It's better to keep your jacket on than to try to move a house by pushing."

Kalman said, "No need to move the old Town Hall. We can take it down board by board. On the other hand, we will have to cut new beams."

Zelig the Bedecked, the mayor of Chelm, was concerned. "Will the new Town Hall look new if we use the old boards?"

"We need a new design, something distinctive," said Naftali the Water Carrier.

"Where will we get a new design?" asked Zalman Shelomo. "There is no master builder in Chelm."

"Pooh! Master builders are no guarantee," said Raisel the Matchmaker. "I heard that Reb Fishel once hired a master builder to make a new office building beside his lumber mill. He hired a builder from Lvov. What a nincompoop that builder was! He designed a nice office building without any windows! Reb Fishel had to hire Chelmers to gather sunlight in sacks to light the inside of his new building."

Dovidl the Nose, Chelm's premiere fisherman, recently appointed to the council of the elders, commented, "You shouldn't believe everything you hear. Someone could be shining you on."

Zelig the Bedecked said, "We should trust in ourselves. We are wise enough to know what is good for us. Come, let us send a couple of men to Brisk and a couple of men to Lvov. They can examine those two Town Halls and tell us what makes each of them distinctive. Then, we will know what to do."

The suggestion was seconded and approved. Ansel the Tinsmith and Anshel, son of Yankel the Tailor, were sent to Lvov on this new mission. To Brisk—since the quickest way to Brisk was by the river—the elders sent two fishermen, Motke Mendel and Havel, son of Shmul the Fishmonger. In a few days, the men returned to Chelm, and the council of elders met to hear their reports.

"The Town Hall in Brisk is made of bricks," reported Motke Mendel. "It is three stories high and you have to climb three steps to reach the door. Two policemen stand on either side of the front door."

"Another thing sets it apart," added Havel. "Near the front steps is a fountain, and in the center of the fountain is a metal fish pointed to the sky with water bubbling out of its mouth."

"The Town Hall in Lvov is wooden like our old Town Hall," reported Anshel. "It is only two stories high, but the first story has a wing with three prison cells. In front of the wing is a wooden gallows with three steps leading to its platform. A rope with a noose dangles in the wind day and night."

Zalman Shelomo smiled. "A warning like that might discourage goniffs," he said, thinking in particular of Gedaliah the Goniff, Chelm's own professional thief, with whom Zalman Shelomo's dealings had always been less than satisfactory.

Ansel added, "The Town Hall in Lvov has a spire above the second story, directly above the door, with a black metal rooster at its top. When the wind changes direction, the rooster turns."

Now that the reports were in, the elders sent out for food and began their deliberation. As usual, it was a debate, harangue, discourse, conversation, dispute, and squabble.

Much wisdom was contributed; much was discarded. Food was regularly consumed to the consternation of Zev the Treasurer who constantly reminded them that so much logic and reasoning was more than the town treasury could afford.

They ruled out the gallows, much to the dismay of Zalman Shelomo. They tried to imagine what rooms they required. Everyone agreed they needed a main hall for council meetings, but beyond that it was difficult to imagine what more was required. The suggestion to add a fireplace for cooking was discarded. Constant availability of food might be a distraction, they reasoned. But that discussion led to another call for food.

In the end, they decided that, for Chelm, a single-story Town Hall would suffice with a main room large enough to contain a town meeting. It was suggested, seconded, and approved that the new Town Hall should have its own outhouse, an improvement sorely needed and sorely missed in the old Town Hall's design. The idea of the outhouse was so popular that the suggestion was made that it be placed in front of the new Town Hall where the fountain stood in Brisk, to serve simultaneously as an outhouse and a monument. This suggestion, though seconded, was defeated. The opposition believed that it might be embarrassing for the town elders to be seen entering and leaving a monument, even if some of them did their best thinking there.

Naftali the Water Carrier was a big proponent of a fountain for the new Town Hall. This, he pointed out, might save him numerous trips to the springs at the foot of the mountain. The others demurred. If Naftali would not be the one to carry the water to the fountain, who would carry it? The idea of a dry fountain was also rejected by a narrow margin.

The notion of a spire was inspiring. It was called to a vote almost at once, even before debate on it could result in a call for food. It was approved with only one abstention (actually three). On behalf of the three sages of the academy, Reb Peretz abstained on the grounds that a spire could be construed as a sign of pride and the Holy Books called for humility. "Perhaps," he suggested, "we should dig a spire-sized hole in front of the new Town Hall to demonstrate the divine humility of Chelm." This was rejected for obvious reasons. A town with so much poverty did not need any reminder to be humble. Besides, there were already enough holes in the main road outside the Town Hall.

The issue now turned on what symbol was most appropriate for Chelm. Brisk had its fish and Lvov had its rooster. What would best symbolize Chelm? What sort of fish, beast, or fowl placed on top of the spire would cause Chelmers to point to the new Town Hall with pride? Dovidl the Nose suggested a statue of Grandfather Pike, the most uncatchable fish in the river. This was rejected on grounds that a fish that seemed more clever than the most clever fisherman of Chelm might cast some doubt on the wisdom of Chelm and its fishermen. A statuette of a chicken was rejected, too. Though Chelm was full of chickens and chicken coops, no one could envision taking pride in a chicken. In quick succession, mice, rats, goats, and oxen were similarly dismissed.

The issue was perplexing, indeed. It required a great deal of consideration, to the exhaustion of all. Reb Feivel, who normally slept in fits and starts during such discussions, and whose snoring sometimes punctuated a vote, suddenly leapt to his feet with an idea. "A plum!" he cried out. His wisdom was unmistakable.

"Of course, a plum!" cried Sissel.

"Nothing says Chelm more than plum pudding, plum schnapps, plump prunes, and plum preserves. Nothing swells a Chelmer with more pride than his plums!" so proclaimed Tzeitel the Butcher's Wife.

And debate suddenly ceased. The new spire of the new Town Hall would be topped with a statue of a plum.

The work of taking down the old building and clearing away its fallen roof was accomplished in only a few weeks. Chelmers volunteered their time, though it was noticed after a week or so that the pile of old boards was not as high as it might be, and a number of repaired houses in Chelm had been fixed with boards that looked suspiciously like they might have come from the old Town Hall. There is a little bit of the thief in everyone, of course, so the elders turned a blind eye to a few missing boards, and no one commented on the cause.

As Kalman the Fixer had foreseen, the old beams were gnawed and chewed. Mice and rats were certainly culprits; even porcupines and raccoons could be partly responsible. New beams would have to be cut from the tall pines near the top of the mountain.

A team of Chelmers, equipped with axes and saws, took on the job. As soon as the first pine was felled, the men were thrilled. A single pine like this would make several standing beams and not a few crossbeams. But it was a day-long struggle to carry the heavy log to the bottom of the mountain. At the bottom, the men were exhausted.

Reb Fishel, owner of Chelm's only lumber mill, was naturally curious to see what was happening. He came to the foot of the mountain just in time to see the exhausted men resting against the enormous log. "It's a mountain," he said to them, pointing out the obvious. "With a little push, logs will roll down a mountain."

The men were thunderstruck by this idea. They could hardly wait to try it out. After all, think of how much labor would be saved and how much more could be accomplished without total exhaustion. So they carried the log back up the mountain and rolled it down. The mountain, being more of a hill than a mountain, was gracious enough to be of service. The log rolled down along the path the men had come up and landed with a satisfying plop at the bottom. The men cheered. It was almost fun. One suggested that they carry the log back up again to see it roll down again, but the idea was nixed as being too labor-intensive. Thanks to Reb Fishel, the logging effort soon came to an end.

Kalman the Fixer emerged as Kalman the Master Builder. He supervised the splitting of the logs, the finishing of the beams, and the cutting of the crossbeams. He showed the men where to cut the notches in the beams and how to match the notches with fittings in the crossbeams. He soon had a skeleton erected.

The elders inspected the framework of the new Town Hall. They walked around thumping the crossbeams and kicking the beams to test their strength. All around, there was praise for Kalman. He was "the good Kalman," "the master craftsman Kalman," "the Kalman of fame." This was all too much for the pitiful Kalman who had begun to weep, who had taken his handkerchief from his back pocket, who was wiping his eyes and blowing his nose.

Raisel the Matchmaker put her arms around Kalman's shoulder. "What is it, dear fellow?" she asked.

He sobbed out his reply, "I never had to fix a spire; I have no idea how to build one."

The elders gathered in a circle around Kalman. They took turns comforting him. In the end, they left it up to him. "Just do the best you can," they urged him.

Kalman straightened his shoulders. He looked around at the other elders. "I'll figure it out," he promised.

While the boards were being attached to the beams and crossbeams, while the interior was being plastered, Ansel the Tinsmith fashioned an impressive plum and presented it to the elders. The roof was affixed and the new Town Hall was polished and painted, outside and in. The townsfolk passed it and marveled. The elders visited it and were happy. Only Kalman kept shaking his head and saying, "Not finished."

Something was happening in Kalman's workshop and no one knew quite what. Among themselves, the elders speculated. It had to be a spire, they thought. Why else had Kalman held back the fine metal plum? What else could it be?

Then, one morning early, Kalman climbed to the top of the courthouse roof and nailed his creation into place. And, to this very day, when you visit the new Town Hall of Chelm, you cannot fail to be impressed by this gracious one-story building topped with a metal plum dangling from a noose on a miniature gallows.

THE TRICKSTER

❊ In the Holy Book, Jacob became a rich man by raising goats for his father-in-law, Laban—the same father-in-law who tricked him into two marriages instead of one; the same father-in-law who tricked him into working fourteen years for two brides instead of seven years for one. When the fourteen years were up, Laban asked Jacob, "What wages should I pay you?" Jacob answered, "No wages." Instead, Jacob wanted a herd of goats of his own. Jacob said he would take none of Laban's most valuable goats, the ones with dark glossy coats. "Give me only the less valuable—the spotted and the speckled goats," said Jacob. Laban agreed, "Take as many of the spotted and speckled goats as you find."

But before Jacob had a chance to examine the herd, Laban the trickster found a way to cheat his son-in-law. He had his shepherds go through the herd and separate out all the spotted and speckled goats. These he moved three days' journey away from his homestead to a place where Jacob would never find them. When Jacob went to separate his goats from Laban's herd, he found none that were speckled or spotted.

Jacob had the last laugh. He mated the remaining goats so cleverly that more and more speckled and spotted ones were born. In a while, his herd grew large and Jacob grew rich at the expense of Laban, whose herd diminished. Thus, the Holy Book teaches, no trickster can succeed against you if God is on your side.

❀ Yankel the Tailor had a goat and his goat died. Obviously, Yankel was not happy that his goat had died. All the same, he was more distraught on account of his mother-in-law, Laylah, who stood for him in the place that Laban stood for our father Jacob, doing everything in her power to harass and provoke him.

"You didn't feed that goat properly," she accused him.

"I know," he answered.

"You let that goat grow skinny and useless. Now you have no goat."

"I know," he said, though he knew the goat had fed well and only lost its normal goatish appetite when it grew old and came close to dying.

"You never respected that goat," Laylah persisted.

"I know," he answered.

"You neglected it and so it died on you. Now you have no goat."

"I know," he said, though he knew he had given that goat love and attention as long as he owned it.

Yankel could also count on his wife Zelda to join in when his mother-in-law got started. Zelda said, "Now there's no milk for the children—no milk for the cheese."

"I know," he answered. "Thank God, we can afford to buy cow's milk from Berel the Dairyman."

Zelda pointed an accusing finger. "Today, you can afford to buy cow's milk! But what if we have a lean season; what if no one needs mending or sewing? What then, my wise Chelmer?"

"It could happen," he admitted sheepishly.

Laylah turned to Zelda. "If only your father were alive. He would know what to do. Curse him for being dead when we need him. There never was a time when that man did not play hard to get."

"Well, he is not here," replied Zelda. She turned to Yankel. "Take the money you think you need to buy cow's milk now. Go to Tishevitz and find that famous goatherd, Gantze Gibor, and buy a nanny goat."

"So far as Tishevitz?" Yankel complained.

"Already, he is turning back!" Laylah remarked.

"To Tishevitz," repeated Zelda. "Everyone knows that the goats of Gantze Gibor are the finest milk goats anywhere."

Yankel had a thought. Walking to Tishevitz might not be such a bad idea. It takes a while to walk there and back and the road passes through Zamosc. He could make it a two days' journey by stopping overnight. So it would be four days before he returned to Chelm. Four days away. Four days without a stitch of work. Four days without Laylah and Zelda. That would be something. So, he answered, "If you insist, I shall go."

As she packed him a few things to eat on the road, Zelda warned him, "Guard your money well. They say that Gantze Gibor is a sharp trader."

"Never you mind," Yankel said, "I myself know how to cut the fabric so more is left for the tailor."

Yankel was feeling good as he passed Zalman Shelomo the Gatekeeper and left the walls of Chelm. He was still feeling good as he stopped under the trees by the side of the road for lunch. And he was feeling light and young when he came to Izzie's Inn and Tavern under the sign of the drunken ox in Zamosc. Here, he stopped for the night, though he could have made most of the distance of Tishevitz by nightfall. Still, a good pull or two on Izzie's famous grain liquor never hurt a man—and a good dinner made by Izzie's wife, Faigeleh, was nothing to sneeze at.

Yankel was not used to drinking, but he did his best, all the while passing his time by chatting with Izzie. To the innkeeper, he confided his mission. He was bound for Gantze Gibor to buy a nanny goat wet as a river. After two drinks, he confided his mission again. Izzie commented that he had best go easy on the drinking until he had some supper.

To give him a "for example," Izzie told him that one day a rabbi came in and saw one of his flock who had been thirsty and was now tipsy. The rabbi scolded him.

"Do not be concerned on my account, dear Rabbi," the drinker said, balancing on his chair and waving his hand. "I am not at all drunk."

"I know drunk when I see it," the rabbi responded, "and how else would you be in this condition?"

The drinker explained: "I took one drink—that's never too much for a good Jew to take. A man is entitled to one drink. After all, imbibing a bit is the best way to see God's world in all its splendor. In fact, one drink of Izzie's schnapps is all it took to make me a new man."

"Come now, you have had more than one drink," scolded the rabbi.

"Oh, that! Dear rabbi, once I was a new man, I was entitled to one drink. So the new man had a drink. Then, there were two of us. Of course, two Jews are permitted to enjoy their companionship with a glass of liquor. So we each had a drink. Those two drinks made us joyous; and, it being a joyous occasion, we called for a bottle!"

Yankel laughed and ordered another drink. He sat down to a fine meal, went up to his room, and fell fast asleep. He awoke the next morning only a little hung over from the night before. And he walked to Tishevitz.

The word *gantze* in Yiddish means "whole" or "complete," as when you have the *gantze megillah*, the "whole story," or a *gantze mensch*, a "complete gentleman." But it can also be used to mean "more than expected." For instance, in Chelm, Zalman Shelomo, a man of great bulk, might be considered gantze. In Tishevitz, if Zalman Shelomo were standing beside Gantze Gibor, he would seem like Gantze Gibor's shadow at midday. Gantze Gibor was a big man. In fact, he had so much substance that another man might be living inside him. Sitting down, he used two chairs and looked like he might have been happier with three.

This made negotiating with Gantze Gibor a daunting affair. Never mind. Yankel was no man to fear circumference. When Yankel saw width, he measured it in fabric; girth to him looked like gold.

"I want a nanny goat that gives milk the way water falls off a mountain," Yankel began.

"So, you have come to Gantze Gibor, which is the right place to come. We have billy goats that never stop breeding until they collapse of exhaustion, and we have nanny goats that give enough milk to fill a lake with what comes out of one nipple on the udder of just one!"

"And the price?"

Gantze Gibor looked wounded. "What lies have you heard? Gantze Gibor never charges more than a fair price! Set your qualms to rest. Let me show you my herd. Choose any one you like. The price is the same no matter which one you choose. I will never have it said in Chelm that Gantze Gibor took advantage of a Chelmer." As he pushed himself off his chairs and stood to his full height, he added, "No matter what people may say of Chelm."

Yankel knew what people in Tishevitz said of Chelm, but he had not come all this way to discuss the foolishness of the Tishevitz folk. So he followed Gantze Gibor out to the herd.

Never had he seen so many beautiful goats in one place. The male goats were in one pen and the female goats in another. Gantze Gibor led him to the pen of the nanny goats. "Pick any one," he said to Yankel.

Now Yankel began to look closely. How would he choose the one he wanted? In addition to being a good milker, it needed some distinguishing mark, some way for him to know it. He thought of his own poor goat that had died so recently. That one he could always know. Some goats are born with a splash of white between their eyes. His old goat had such a marking, and he saw that there were a few in the herd of Gantze Gibor that also had it.

"I want one with white on its face," Yankel said.

"White like milk," said Gantze Gibor. "A good way to choose." And he turned to one of the goatherds standing nearby. "Fetch the best nanny with a white face for this friend of ours from Chelm. Make sure it is one that gives much milk."

The goatherd brought a nanny goat to Yankel. In the meantime, Yankel and Gantze Gibor had negotiated a price. "This one will do," said the big man. "But, listen to me. Spend the night here in Tishevitz. Come back in the morning and see her milked. You will see that you are getting the best nanny your money can buy."

That's how it was left. Yankel spent the night at an inn in Tishevitz. The liquor was not as good as the whiskey of Izzie and the food was not as good as the cooking of Faigeleh, but he was rested the next morning nonetheless.

"Now you shall see for yourself," Gantze Gibor greeted him. And there was the nanny he had chosen and the milking stool. And Yankel watched as the goatherd milked and milked. Three pails overflowing with milk! He paid Gantze Gibor, who gave him the goat on a leash, and he headed for Chelm with a broad smile on his face. It had all gone so well and been so painless. And he still could look forward to a night at Izzie's Inn and Tavern.

He alternately sang to himself and whistled a tune until he came to the inn in the afternoon. He asked Izzie's son to put the goat in the stable and feed it. He was staying overnight. Then Yankel went in and ordered his drink. "Heaven," he thought.

"How did it go with Gantze Gibor?" Izzie asked.

"What a goat he sold me! I saw it milked this morning. Pails and pails of milk she gave. I cannot wait to see my wife's face when she milks this nanny!"

So they spoke and Faigeleh overheard. And Faigeleh thought, "A goat like that should belong to an innkeeper's wife, not to a tailor." And Faigeleh thought, "Perhaps I could trade his nanny for one of mine, for my nannies are no champions when it comes to giving milk."

Faigeleh slipped out and looked at the nanny tied in the stable, contentedly chewing on straw. "Too bad," she thought. "None of my nanny goats has a white flame on its forehead." Then Faigeleh thought, "I do have a billy goat with a white forehead." And Faigeleh thought, "And this tailor is from Chelm. Perhaps I could switch my billy goat for his nanny goat and he would not even notice." And that is what Faigeleh did.

The next morning, she led the billy goat out of the barn on the leash that belonged to the nanny. "Here is your goat," said Faigeleh.

Yankel, feeling well fed and well rested, said, "Thank you again for your wonderful food." He took the leash from Faigeleh, patted the goat affectionately on the head, and set out for Chelm.

As he came within earshot of his tailor's shop, he called out, "Zelda! Come and see what I have brought you! A nanny goat from Gantze Gibor, but what a nanny goat! This one could fill the whole land of milk and honey and make it a land where you could not fit any honey!"

Zelda came outside to see the new goat, and her mother Laylah followed right behind. Little Chaya, their daughter, came next, followed by Yankel's eldest, Anshel. "Look," cried Little Chaya, "it has a star on its head just like our old goat."

"Yes, yes!" said Yankel. He turned to Anshel and said, "Bring a milking stool so your mother can see what a fine investment I have made for her."

"It will do no good," said Anshel.

"What do you mean?" Yankel demanded.

"This goat is a billy goat," said Anshel, pointing to the obvious. "I do not think you will get any milk from a billy."

Zelda bent over, looked, stood upright, and put her hands to her face. Laylah looked and said, "You have been swindled.

Of course, you have been swindled. Didn't I warn you to watch out for your money?"

Yankel was beside himself. Why, only that morning, the goat had been milked. He got down on all fours beside the goat to look for himself. There was no denying the fact that this was a billy goat.

"Turn around at once," commanded Zelda, "and get that cheat Gantze Gibor to give you a nanny goat that is a nanny goat."

Yankel said, "I'm tired. Let me rest. I'll start out again in the morning."

"Nothing of the sort!" said Zelda, and she crossed her arms across her chest.

Yankel knew better than to argue with that. He led the goat by its leash and walked until he came to Izzie's Inn and Tavern. Faigeleh had finished serving supper, and she was sitting on the porch. She came down to greet him, "You are back with your goat?"

Yankel explained what had happened, how he had been cheated by Gantze Gibor, how his wife had sent him back. He handed the leash to Faigeleh, saying, "Please feed this goat and keep it in the barn. In the morning, I will take it back to Gantze Gibor and there will be sparks flying, I promise you."

Faigeleh took the goat. And Faigeleh thought, "If Gantze Gibor sees a billy goat, he will know that something has gone wrong. It will not take him long to add two and two and come up with me." And Faigeleh thought, "I will switch the goats again. The man from Chelm will never check."

So it was. In the morning, Faigeleh presented the goat on the leash to Yankel and Yankel set off for Tishevitz. He found Gantze Gibor sitting on his chairs, as if he had never left him.

"Do you take me for a fool?" he shouted. "Why did you give me a billy goat instead of a nanny? Do you cheat all your customers?"

"Calm down, little Chelmer, you are speaking to Gantze Gibor, and I never cheat a customer, and I never give a nanny for a billy or a billy for a nanny."

"You did this time," Yankel insisted.

Gantze Gibor pushed himself up, approached the goat, and said, "Yes, I recognize this goat. This is the goat I sold you, one of my best milkers."

Lo and behold, when one of the goatherds arrived with pails and milk stool, Yankel could only stare as his goat happily was relieved of two pailfuls of milk. Gantze Gibor went back to sit down.

"My deepest apology," said Yankel. "I do not know what happened. Back in Chelm, this goat was a billy goat. Here, it is a nanny goat."

"No matter what they say about Chelm," said Gantze Gibor, thoughtfully, "I certainly thought a Chelmer could tell a nanny goat from a billy goat."

So it was that Yankel turned around again and headed for home, stopping only at Izzie's Inn and Tavern for a drink and a meal. So it was that Faigeleh again switched goats on him. So it was that he reached home again triumphant, only to find that his nanny goat was again a billy goat. So it was that Zelda sent him back to Tishevitz to face the formidable Gantze Gibor. So it was that Yankel stopped again at the Inn and the switch was made again. So it was that when he faced Gantze Gibor and accused him, the goat turned out to be a nanny goat again.

This time, Yankel demanded proof that the goat was a nanny, proof that he could show to his wife and to his mother-in-law.

Gantze Gibor was not dismayed. "The best proof is the milk," he said. "But for a Chelmer, we will go out of our way." They sent for the rabbi of Tishevitz. Gantze Gibor had the nanny goat milked before the eyes of the rabbi and Yankel and all the goatherds. Then the rabbi wrote out a certificate

stating that the goat that Gantze Gibor sold to Yankel the
Tailor of Chelm was a bona fide nanny goat.

Yankel tucked the certificate into his jacket pocket,
thanked Gantze Gibor, thanked the rabbi of Tishevitz, and
walked the goat back to Izzie's Inn, where he told the whole
story to Izzie. Faigeleh overheard everything and could
hardly restrain herself. She wanted so badly to laugh out
loud that she ran into the barn, where she laughed as she
changed the leash from the nanny goat to the billy goat, and
laughed as she tied the billy goat in the nanny goat's place.

The next morning, Faigeleh, straining to maintain a
straight face, again presented the goat to Yankel.

Yankel again walked back to Chelm, stopping from time
to time to be sure that he had the certificate secure in his
pocket. He sat beneath a tree just to close his eyes for a little
nap. He was so tired of all the walking from Chelm to Zamosc,
from Zamosc to Tishevitz, from Tishevitz to Zamosc, and
from Zamosc to Chelm, that he did not notice when the leash
slipped out of his hand as he nodded off. The goat did as goats
will do, foraging from bush to bush, eating leaves off low
branches, and then eating the low branches. It wandered as
goats will wander.

When Yankel awoke, he checked to be sure he had the
certificate. Then he looked around. The goat had vanished.
He searched and searched but could not find it. It grew dark
and he grew frantic, but there was no sign of the goat. It was
night when he pounded on the gate of Chelm until a tired
Zalman Shelomo let him in.

Yankel thought to himself, "Zelda will have to make do
with the certificate. She will complain, of course. Her mother
will complain, of course. I'll accept the blame, of course. I
have lost the goat and I have wasted the money. What can I
do? At least, I have the certificate."

All this transpired, but it is not the end of the story. The
billy goat ate its way home to Izzie's Inn and Tavern. Izzie
saw it grazing on the grass in front of the porch and he

thought, "How did my goat get loose?" He took it by the leash and led it back to the barn. What did he see? He saw double. Here were two identical goats, both with flames on their forehead. Surely, only one of these was his. He looked more closely and the truth came over him like a splash of cold water. He shook his head and called his wife Faigeleh. "You have been up to mischief," he admonished her.

Faigeleh was honest, at least with her husband. "Look at it this way," she said. "The tailor from Chelm needed a nanny, and we needed a nanny. He needed a nanny for his family, but our need was greater. So I traded a goat for a goat. How could I know that the billy goat would come back?"

Izzie was angry. "If you needed a new nanny goat, why not tell me?"

❊ The next day, back in Chelm, Yankel was in his tailor shop, mending clothes. He had tacked the certificate from the rabbi of Tishevitz on the wall where he could keep an eye on it. How many times had he told his wife that the rabbi of Tishevitz was no liar and no cheat? Yankel had witnessed it all for himself. In Tishevitz, the goat had been a nanny. True, in Chelm, it had been a billy goat, but the certificate was genuine, written on parchment (and parchment is not cheap). So, at least, he had the rabbi's word to show for all his travails.

Yankel's mother-in-law still complained what a worthless fellow he was, how he was gulled, and how she warned him. His wife was not speaking to him at all.

But Little Chaya went out to play and came running back into the shop, yelling, "It's the goat! The goat is back!"

Everyone ran outside. Lo, there was the goat tied to the fence beside the house. Yankel stood back. He was afraid to look too closely. He asked himself, "Does it make any difference what kind of goat it is this time?" His son, Anshel, bent down and peeked.

"Ho, ho!" Anshel said. "Now I will fetch a milking stool and a pail."

Yankel patted the goat on its head and sighed, "Thank God, it's over."

It was not quite over. The story of Yankel and the goat was told and retold in Chelm, and always with the same ending. Yankel the Tailor had the wisest goat in Chelm. It was wise enough to be both a billy and a nanny, whichever it pleased. And it was wise enough not only to find its own way home but to tie its own leash to Yankel's fence. Everyone agreed: "That Gantze Gibor of Tishevitz knew goats! His were always the best."

THE PEARL

✿ Usually, Hirschel the Wood Carrier cut wood from the forest outside Chelm. One winter's day, however, he chose not to leave Chelm but to take wood from the grove of trees near the base of the hill known as Chelm's mountain. From here, trips to The Hill to deliver firewood to the wealthy would be shorter. Plenty of good branches were within reach. Hirschel chopped until he had a nice-sized pile at hand, whereupon he bent to wrap them in his fabric carrying-sling. It was then that he spied, out of the corner of his eye, a shiny object.

His mind flashed to Moses—the shepherd who noticed something small and extraordinary and turned aside to discover the burning bush. Here was Hirschel, like Moses, turning aside. But this little glint of light, half covered in dirt, was no flaming revelation. As soon as he had it in his hand, though he had never before held one in his life, Hirschel knew it was an outsized, iridescent pearl—smooth, alluring, satisfying to touch. He used his sleeve to brush the earth off it; then he closed his hand around it.

Hirschel could have pocketed the pearl. Perhaps it would make him rich enough to buy his own house on The Hill so that he could order wood from some other wood carrier. On the other hand, if he were suddenly rich, his friends would wonder whether all these years Hirschel had been swindling them. They would be asking one another, "Did Hirschel overcharge us? Was he dishonest?" The thought brought such a bad taste to his mouth that he had to spit.

"Anyway," Hirschel thought, "this land rightfully belongs to the village of Chelm. Some Chelmer must have lost the pearl. Pearls don't just pop up." Then he asked himself, "Where do pearls pop up from?" He had no idea. On the other hand, if it had been lost by some Chelmer, that Chelmer would be looking for it. And, if it had been lost by some stranger who had abandoned the search for it, the Holy Books ruled that the pearl would belong to the town. For now, he plopped the pearl into his pocket and went on gathering branches to carry them up to The Hill.

That evening, when work was done, he sought out Zelig the Bedecked, the mayor of Chelm. Hirschel found him in the tavern and sat down across from him at the table. "Buy me a drink," Hirschel said, "and I will share with you a secret."

His drink arrived. With an air of drama, he reached into his pocket and spread out his handkerchief on the table, carefully placing the pearl in its center. Zelig the Bedecked stared. After a breathless moment, Zelig reached out and touched the pearl with the tip of his forefinger. It rolled a little beneath his touch. "Where did this come from?" he asked. And Hirschel the Wood Carrier told him everything.

The next morning, the elders met in the new Town Hall. While the rabbi slept in his chair, snoring now and then, the elders discussed the pearl. No one could remember such a thing, and there was no record of any pearl in Chelm's official annals. The morning passed and the elders reached only one conclusion. The pearl must belong to someone, though no one had reported it missing. Speculation was that it rolled to the base of the mountain from The Hill, but why had none of the wealthy Chelmers complained of its loss?

The elders ordered that the ground around where the pearl had been found should be searched. It had not yet snowed in Chelm that year, and it had been a while since the last rain, so the ground was cold but dry. If an animal had left the pearl, or some traveler had dropped it, there might be traces. Hirschel was nominated to lead the search party.

Hirschel had been in possession of the pearl up to this point, but now Zev the Treasurer took charge of it on behalf of the village. Hirschel relinquished it with reluctance. He had so much enjoyed the feel of it when he put his hand into his pocket. No matter. His was a lonely profession, so he looked forward to leading the search team and having some company for a change. To conduct the search, the elders selected Tzeitel the Butcher's Wife (for her sharp vision), Kalman the Fixer (for his attention to detail), Sissel (for her sweet and peerless tzimmes), and Naftali the Water Carrier (for his fluid thinking) to join Hirschel.

The searchers reached the spot Hirschel remembered in mid-afternoon. On a cursory look-around, nothing stood out, so they spread themselves in a line to walk toward the mountain. Close to the point at which the mountain's slope rose, Tzeitel shrieked, "Another one! I found another pearl!" Almost immediately, Naftali also found a pearl and called out, "Here's another!" The search team now closed in on the area between Tzeitel and Naftali. Heads down and senses alert, they walked step-by-step up the gentle rise. Lo and behold, nearly hidden in the brush was the petite mouth of a cave and just this side of the entrance was... another pearl. Hirschel spied them both—cave and pearl—and called the others to join him.

One by one, the members of the team peered into the hole to no avail. It was nothing but blackness inside—too dark for any human eye. Moreover, the opening itself was too small to enter. They would have to return with someone smaller and thinner than any of them. To prevent anyone else from finding it in the meantime, Kalman gathered brush and arranged it to cover the hole.

As the searchers returned to the new Town Hall, they conferred and agreed that the pearls they found had led like a trail straight to the little mouth in the mountain. More than that, it was difficult to say.

Ah, the avarice of mankind. Presented with the three additional pearls, the elders were ready, indeed eager, to mount a major expedition, even to dig up the entire mountain, if necessary, to find more of these translucent baubles. Hirschel raised his hands to quiet them, to remind them that they were not ordinary treasure hounds.

"My friends," he said. "As elders of Chelm, we must proceed with wisdom, not haste. Clearly, the pearls led to the cave. But it seems obvious that this is not a case of singular pearls popping off the mountain, but of pearls which somehow rolled downhill from that cave."

Reb Feivel had just awakened, refreshed from his catnap. He perked up his head. "I think I understand what Hirschel means," he said. "The cave must be a pearl mine!"

Dovidl the Nose, the fisherman recently called to serve as an elder, said, "Reb Feivel, I beg to differ with you. Sailors tell of oysters giving pearls."

Naftali asked, "Mayhap, oysters swallow pearls that come from pearl mines?"

Dovidl the Nose shrugged his shoulders.

Hirschel said, "We should inspect the cave and find out for ourselves."

The very next day, the search party, joined by Havel, the young and thin son of Shmul the Fishmonger, made its way to the opening. They carried a long coil of rope and a small hand lantern, the kind used by travelers for night walks. Kalman cleared away the branches and leaves from the cave's mouth. One end of the rope was tied to a stout tree close by, and the other end was wrapped around Havel's waist. Havel cinched it with a sturdy sailor's knot. The lantern was lit by lifting the hinged portion of its lid and touching the stubby candle within with a piece of kindling.

The opening was a tight fit even for lean, little Havel. But he squirmed into the hole, and half a body length later, the cave widened. Its measure from bottom to top was sufficient for Havel to stand though his head almost touched the ceiling. As Havel stood, the light of the lantern slowly infused the entire cave. Now he could see the cave well enough to know that, standing in the center, he could stretch out his arms in every direction without touching a side. Only a dozen steps into the mountain, though, the cave abruptly ended.

Havel called out to the waiting elders, "This is no pearl mine." Then he turned to examine the interior. The floor and ceiling were bare, as were all the walls except for the far wall. Havel held the lantern closer and saw that at the back wall someone had gone to a lot of trouble. A long ledge had been carved into the wall, big enough for a man to use as a bed. There was something at one end of the ledge that looked like a pillow, but when Havel reached out and pulled at it, he heard it rattle and clink. It was a bag made of sackcloth, full of some noisy "somethings."

Havel raised the lantern to check the candle. There was not much left of it. He realized that his expedition to the cave's interior was near its end. So he dragged the sack close to the cave's mouth. Using his remaining light, he removed the rope from his waist and knotted it around the top end of the sack.

The search party was waiting for him as Havel slithered out of the cave, blinked, and rubbed his eyes. Kalman helped Havel pull on the rope that was still stretched into the cave, and behold, the sack squeezed through the cave's mouth emitting a slight popping sound as it emerged and jangling when it fell to the ground. Havel smiled. "Not a pearl mine," he said, "but just maybe we have found a treasure. I think we stumbled onto a thief's lair, maybe the hideout of Gedaliah the Goniff."

The bag was dutifully carried unopened to the new Town Hall. It was set down in the middle of the room and Havel brought out the items in it, one by one. "The gold buttons from my sweater," said Tzeitel, amazed to see them again. "My grandfather's snuff box," said Zev. "I thought I lost it last winter in the snow." All Chelm soon heard what was transpiring, and the Chelmers gathered to witness the spectacle. Pins, rings, collars of lace, candlesticks, cups for blessing Sabbath wine, silver bracelets, kitchen curtains, children's dolls, prayer books, hair combs, mirrors, and amulets emerged from the bag.

"I thought I lost this forever."

"I thought I dropped this in the mud."

"I thought the wind took these from my laundry line."

Piece by piece, everything was claimed, except for the very last thing in the very bottom of the sack: another lustrous pearl, a perfect match for the four pearls that had somehow fallen to make the trail that led Hirschel and his team to the cave. It was bad luck for Gedaliah the Goniff but good luck for the village of Chelm, especially since no one had come forward to claim the pearls. Zev the Treasurer held the five round gems high in his palm and said, "Chelm is rich beyond imagining!"

Zalman Shelomo the Gatekeeper, and the closest thing Chelm had to a policeman, said, "Now we can build a prison with iron bars."

Yankel the Tailor said, "Now we can afford to buy fabric and sew drapes for the new Town Hall."

Raisel the Matchmaker said, "Now we can afford dowries for every young maiden in Chelm."

Sissel, who owned the café, said, "Now we elders can send out for better food."

Tzeitel the Butcher's Wife said, "Now everyone in Chelm can afford to buy meat."

Kalman the Fixer said, "Now we can afford a metal lock for the city gate."

Zelig the Bedecked, the mayor of Chelm, said, "Now we can make a sign in big letters near the top of the hill spelling out 'CHELM' so people can look up and know where they are."

Reb Feivel, the Glory of Chelm, said, "Now we can buy a new Eternal Light for the synagogue. The old one is not as eternal as it once was."

But Zev the Treasurer said, "Chelmers, the pearls are priceless, but they are not gold. We cannot spend pearls."

The issue now was how to turn the pearls into gold or silver. The elders sent out for food and began to debate. The plan was so simple it was concocted after only two days of haggling, haranguing, wrangling, and quibbling. They would send Zev the Treasurer and Hirschel the Wood Carrier to the celebrated market of Tishevitz. There, and only there, would they surely find a merchant wealthy enough to afford such pearls.

The very next day, the two set out. In recognition of his part in finding the pearls, Zev permitted Hirschel to carry one in his pocket. Hirschel was thrilled each time he put his hand there to touch and turn that exquisite prize. The two elders stopped overnight at Izzie's Inn and Tavern (beneath the sign of the drunken ox) to sample Izzie's outstanding whiskey and savor the incomparable fare prepared by Izzie's wife, Faigeleh. Of their mission, they said not a word. They knew that brigands sometimes posed as travelers at the inns to determine who it might be worthwhile to waylay the next day. A stray comment, innocent or accidental, even between honest people, might be overheard and result in disaster.

The following day, Zev and Hirschel reached the market at Tishevitz. Since Yankel the Tailor swore by the honesty of Gantze Gibor, the two Chelmers went directly to his stall. They found him seated on two chairs in the midst of a bevy of goats and sheep being tended by two of his shepherds. As they had agreed in advance, Zev showed him only one pearl. The big man was impressed.

"Take my advice," said Gantze Gibor, "invest it in sheep. You will never regret it. Sheep are gold on the hoof. They give you the wool off their backs and bear interest every spring in the form of more sheep for the flock. With sheep, you can never go wrong. But if you are determined to sell your pearl for gold, go to the shop of Reuven the Assayer. He buys and sells gold. Reuven is a God-fearing man; he will give you proper value."

They located the shop of Reuven the Assayer. Above was a sign displaying a painted golden scale. They felt secure that they had come to the right place. Again, Zev showed only one pearl. Reuven looked at it through an eyepiece made of thick glass. Hirschel asked if he could look at it through the eyepiece, too, and Reuven allowed him to do so. How close the eyepiece brought the pearl! How smooth the surface and how it shined! Hirschel handed the eyepiece and the pearl back to Reuven, who passed the pearl to his assistant to weigh it and measure it. "You have a stunning pearl," he said. These were his only words. The assistant came back with the pearl and four bags of gold coins.

"Thank you for your offer," said Zev. "And, just supposing we had another pearl like that, would the price be the same?"

"The same," Reuven said, nodding and tilting his head to take a second look at the two Chelmers standing before him. Did he wonder if they had found a pearl mine?

But the two Chelmers, pearl in hand, stepped just outside the assay shop to talk it over. If one pearl were worth four bags of gold coins, then they were faced with the prospect of carrying twenty bags of gold coins back to Chelm. There was no possibility that the two of them could manage to carry so much without help. Then, too, even with help, carrying that much gold in sacks would make them a target for every thief from Tishevitz to Zamosc and from Zamosc to Chelm.

"We could sell one pearl and go home," said Hirschel. "If we walk straight through, never stopping, we might be safe."

"Or we could sell one pearl and buy a donkey cart and a barrel," Zev suggested, thinking out loud. "We could then sell the other pearls and put the gold coins in the barrel to disguise them as fish or whiskey or wine. Thieves are less likely to steal a barrel than bags of coins."

They went back into the assay shop and sold one pearl. Taking the gold coins, they went to the blacksmith and bought a likely-looking donkey and a cart that had seen better days. They did not buy the best cart since they did not wish to look too prosperous. And they did not choose the best donkey for the same reason. The barrel maker sold them a used barrel redolent with the sickly-sweet odor of stale marsh mallow. They bought straw in the market mainly as food for the donkey. This, they were convinced, was perfect.

They parked their cart and donkey with its straw and barrel on board in front of Reuven's assay shop. Imagine Reuven's surprise when the two Chelmers produced three more pearls to sell him. True to form, Reuven was undaunted. He studied each pearl and had his assistant weigh and measure each one. "Fine pearls," he said. The result was his ready offer of twelve bags of gold coins for the three pearls. He smiled and shook hands with Zev and with Hirschel. Reuven seemed as pleased with the pearls as they were with the coins.

Do not be confused, Dear Reader. Some people imagine that Chelmers are not good at mathematics. One story tells how a dismayed young man came to the rabbi of Chelm saying he had been married only three months and his wife had given birth to a baby daughter. "*Mazel tov*, congratulations," the rabbi responded, then asked: "So what is your problem?"

The young man said, "Rabbi, it is only that I have been told it takes nine months to have a baby."

"True," the rabbi answered, "and you say you have been married three months?"

"Yes."

"And your wife has also been married three months?"

"Yes."

"So you have been together three months?"

"Yes, Rabbi."

"Well, there is your answer," the rabbi concluded. "Three months and three months and three months is nine months. Go home and enjoy your daughter." Proof that Chelmers have no problem with mathematics!

The truth is that Hirschel had convinced Zev they should sell only four of the pearls. The fifth one should be held in reserve in case of an emergency. Hirschel failed to make clear what kind of emergency or how he would use the fifth one without trading it for gold coins, but he was so vehement and so determined to hold back one pearl that Zev gave in. The pearl in Hirschel's pocket remained in Hirschel's pocket.

Fifteen bags of coins were stacked in the barrel, padded beneath and between by straw. More straw covered them to the barrel's top. Then the lid was placed and the barrel was hammered shut. What remained of the sixteenth sack was held by Zev the Treasurer for expenses along the way, though it was obviously too much for any expenses, but who could tell? Hirschel and Zev agreed that it was burden enough for the donkey to bear the weight of the barrel, so they walked along beside the cart.

Halfway to Zamosc, the donkey stopped and refused to go any farther. They took it out of the cart's traces, and tied it to a tree by the side of the road. Together, Zev and Hirschel managed to pull the cart off the road near where the donkey was tethered. They put down some straw for the donkey to eat. But now they were worried. They agreed the donkey should rest awhile, but they wondered if this was going to become a pattern. Every minute they were on the road was another minute to worry. Every passerby might be a highwayman—the women might even be highwaywomen! Every shadow from the trees near the road could spell danger. Their eyes never left the barrel, even as they attempted to look casual and unconcerned.

An hour later, the donkey seemed willing to move again. They strapped it into the traces and continued on their way. But the old cart somehow found a deep rut in the road and this caused a crack to appear above the axle. Now the cart was sometimes riding above the axle, as it should, and sometimes scraping the axle, as it should not. The barrel would shift when the scraping occurred, and each time the cart had to be stopped to center the barrel. By the time they pulled in to Izzie's Inn and Tavern, they were exhausted. They were worried about leaving the cart with its precious cargo so they took turns going into the inn to eat. Then they were worried that they seemed too concerned about the barrel; surely someone would become suspicious.

Zev and Hirschel debated and considered. Perhaps Gantze Gibor had been right in the first place. If only they had traded the pearls for sheep and goats, they would have had an easier time. But then, if they had traded for sheep and goats, they would have had to hire shepherds to help drive them. And the sheep and goats would have strayed on to many farms and into many fields along the way, so that they would be constantly stopping just to pay for the damage being done by the animals. No, sheep and goats would not have been any more practical than the donkey and barrel. Before they concluded this, they had taken turns several times going into Izzie's Inn and Tavern and having a drink. Each drink helped them think a little more clearly.

Three things happened which made up their minds. First, they agreed without any dissent that they needed a lighter cargo for the donkey and cart. Something light and valuable had to be found quickly; otherwise, the cart would never make it all the way to Chelm.

Second, between the cart and the outhouse behind Izzie's Inn and Tavern, there was a coop of chickens and geese. On his return from one trip, Zev suggested that chickens were, of course, smaller than sheep and might do much less damage. Hirschel said, sensibly, that no one could herd chickens as far as Chelm, so they would have to be in cages. In between another series of drinks, they tried to calculate the number of chickens that they could buy with fifteen sacks of gold coins. (It was a prodigious number to calculate even for Zev.) Then they tried to imagine how many cages they would be able to put on the cart and how much weight the donkey would be able to pull. They next considered selling the donkey and the cart to buy an ox and a four-wheeler oxcart. By this point, their heads were whirling with calculations (and also with the fine schnapps offered in the inn beneath the sign of the drunken ox). Then Hirschel said something inspired: "If chickens are lighter than gold and can be just as precious, feathers are even lighter than chickens." They drank to this insight, the drinking made easier since they stopped going into Izzie's Inn for one drink at a time and bought a couple of bottles to share outside beside the cart and barrel. In the meantime, they put down straw for the donkey and ordered some good feed grain from Faigeleh. After all, if they were going to drink grain, the donkey should, at least, have a taste, too.

When, on one of his now frequent visits to the back, Zev met Faigeleh near the chicken coop, he offered to buy as many feathers as she could produce. After all, she plucked feathers from birds before she cooked them. Faigeleh told Zev that chicken feathers were not worth much, but she could offer him truly valuable feathers, goose and duck. Zev told her he had gold coins to trade for all the goose and duck feathers she could find. Faigeleh told Zev to wait by the cart.

In a short while, Faigeleh and her son and two daughters came out of the inn carrying stacks of pillows. Pillows! This was better than anything Hirschel and Zev could imagine. Pillows would be light enough to carry on the cart, light enough for the donkey to pull. Faigeleh and her children stacked the pillows beside the cart. Zev paid her a gold coin for every small pillow and two gold coins for every large pillow. Faigeleh, being nobody's fool, knew a good deal when she had one. "We have some feather mattresses," she said.

"Bring them on!" said Hirschel euphorically.

A dozen feather mattresses soon materialized. Zev counted out seven gold coins for each mattress. Faigeleh, putting the heavy coins in her apron, asked, "Do you want to buy more?" Zev looked in the barrel. Of course, he still had plenty of gold coins. "Yes," he said, "more feathers! More of those delightfully light feathers" Hirschel said, "but only the good ones, please, duck and goose."

"Of course," Faigeleh replied. Now Faigeleh and her children took the gold coins they had and went from door to door in Zamosc buying more pillows. They paid half a coin for every small pillow and a coin for every large one. They returned and sold the same pillows to Zev and Hirschel for double.

The third thing happened while Zev and Hirschel were busy becoming pillow merchants. The evening breeze came up, as it did every evening around this time. Zev automatically licked his finger and stuck it in the air to see which way the wind was blowing. After a couple more drinks, he said to Hirschel, "Too bad we cannot ride the wind, for it is blowing directly toward Chelm." Suddenly, the full plan came together.

They could not ride the wind, but feathers could ride the wind. This was the stroke of genius that made everything before it seem perfectly reasonable. All night long, the breeze blew. All night long, the two companions tore open pillows and mattresses, releasing the feathers into the wind. No doubt the Chelmers would know what to do with this windfall. Even now, they were probably gathering the feathers! And the two paused long enough to toast their inspiration with a drink before they continued tearing pillows.

The next morning, they loaded the cart with empty pillowcases and mattress sacks. Then they climbed aboard and started off for Chelm, imagining a royal reception. Twice the donkey stopped and had to be rested. At times, the grinding of the cart against the axle made them nervous. But everything held together enough to carry them through the gates of Chelm and right up to the porch of the new Town Hall.

The elders had been informed that Zev and Hirschel were approaching, and they were waiting inside the Town Hall. Zelig the Bedecked, the mayor of Chelm, invited them to come up to speak. The other elders sat attentive. Ah, the fortune they imagined!

Zev asked, "Have you collected all the feathers?"

The elders sat mystified. Feathers?

Hirschel elaborated, "The feathers. The duck feathers. The goose feathers. They were worth a fortune. Did you collect them all?"

There was a deeper and more intense silence than there had been in anticipation. Zev and Hirschel looked at one another and shook their heads.

"Let me put this another way," offered Zev. "Have the feathers we sent from Zamosc reached Chelm?"

There was a kind of "no" on every lip. The elders looked at one another and shook their heads.

So Zev and Hirschel presented a full account of everything that had transpired from the time they left Chelm to the time they returned. And each of them repeated the same thing twice, "The feathers were in the breeze, and the breeze was headed directly for Chelm."

Reb Feivel rose to his feet. "Feathers are very light," he observed. "That may be why the two of you arrived before the feathers."

"Then we can expect the feathers to arrive at any time!" said Zelig the Bedecked.

"At any time," agreed Hirschel. "In the meantime, we did keep one of the pearls in reserve, just in case of emergency." Upon which, he removed the pearl from his pocket and gave it to Zev for safekeeping.

There was not a single elder who was not impressed by this act of foresight. The pearl was, after all, a village treasure. Having it meant that the elders could go on dreaming of what Chelm needed and would someday possess.

But while they are waiting for the feathers to arrive, the elders have agreed not to sell the pearl, but to keep it safe, just in case of an emergency.

THE THREE SAGES

❊ The academy of Chelm, 1½ Chandler Street, occupied a wood-frame building along Chelm's northern wall. Next door to the academy, beneath the sign of the braided candle, was 1 Chandler Street, where Saul the Chandler offered candles and soap. (The street took its name from the chandlery.) Number 2 Chandler Street, on the other side of the academy, belonged to Velvel the Cobbler. On his door there was a sandal attached to a hemp rope. Pulling the sandal rang the cobbler's bell. The academy had no sign and no bell, nothing to indicate from the outside what went on inside.

Three notable sages shared the academy of Chelm and each was the headmaster of his own department. The first was Reb Feibush of Lublin. None now lived who remember when Reb Feibush arrived, but as it sometimes happens, a person and a place may be so compatible that they are like the beginning and the end of a legend. So it was with Reb Feibush and his adopted Chelm. The second was Reb Mendel of Apt. He, too, had been at the academy as long as anyone could recall, and he, too, was accepted by the Chelmers as if he were native-born. The third was Reb Peretz of Ponder. He was not quite as old as his brother sages, though he was surely becoming older by the day. Also unlike them, he was not named for the city of his birth. For years, Chelmers have meticulously read every signpost for quite a distance from Chelm without ever finding a pointer to Ponder. So Reb

Peretz of Ponder must have achieved his appellation through diligent and persistent thought.

As to the departments of the academy of Chelm, probably nowhere in the long and honored tradition of Jewish schooling was there such a perspicacious demarcation of the spheres of knowledge as the three sages had devised at the academy of Chelm. The Division of Highbrow Scholarship was headed by Reb Feibush of Lublin; Reb Mendel of Apt was headmaster of the Division of Advanced Amazement; and Reb Peretz of Ponder was headmaster of the Division of Dire Probity.

One further, yet striking, thing set the academy of Chelm apart from any competitor. It had no students. This fact achieved for the academy its renown as a fine school, a school where no one failed, a school where no student was turned away, a school where no parent had any reason for complaint, and a school where no subject went unlearned.

The three sages were aware, of course, that other scholars made their living by accepting tuition from students. This, they averred, ran counter to the demand of the Holy Books, in which it was written, "You shall not make the Torah into a spade to dig with." Since "the Torah" in this commandment meant the whole panoply of Jewish knowledge, and since "spade" in this commandment meant a tool such as a tradesman employed, and since "to dig with" in this commandment meant to earn a living, the sages saw no honor in accepting money for teaching what they knew.

When they were not attending sessions of the council of Chelm's elders, they practiced their arts in the academy, honing their skills against one another, and answering questions brought to them by Chelmers. A question posed to one of them was posed to them all. In practice, questions were handed from one division to another until a conclusion was advanced, the conclusion then being examined by one division after another until it was pronounced satisfactory, upon which there might still be cause for a minority opinion to be expressed and recorded.

❄ One such case, perhaps the best-known, was brought by Berel the Dairyman.

"My customers complain that my butter is too heavy," Berel began, "but butter should be heavy, else it is not butter. They complain that when they butter a slice of bread and drop it, it always falls to ground on the side that is buttered. How shall I answer them?"

Reb Peretz of Ponder took up the issue. "The question should be considered thoroughly," he said, "starting with the bread." So saying, he sliced a hefty piece of black bread, placed it in the middle of the table, cupped his head in his hands, and directed a steady gaze at the slice.

Suddenly, his concentration was broken by Reb Mendel—thereby, the impetus passed from the Division of Dire Probity to the Division of Advanced Amazement—as Reb Mendel raised a finger high in the air, raised up one foot in memory of the great sage, Hillel, who had stood on one foot whenever answering a question, and cried out, "Aha!"

In any other division of the academy such an emphatic action would be accompanied by some comment on the issue at hand. But the Division of Advanced Amazement did not condone such plebian intellectualism. For Reb Mendel, the exclamation itself had the force of an answer.

"I see what you are saying," Reb Feibush said to Reb Mendel, "and you are on the right track. Leave this question to me for a moment." In this fashion, the question passed to the Division of Highbrow Scholarship.

Now here was something wondrous to behold, for Reb Feibush had the face of a Chinese Shar Pei (though he himself had never seen or heard of that domestic marvel). And, although most writers (and some readers) cringe when encountering a description that interrupts the narrative by comparing things in the telling with things that those in the telling could not conceivably know, there is no other comparison that will do justice at present. Far away, in China, God had endowed the face of the Shar Pei dog with so many loose folds of skin that not only was the face expressive, but the skin itself was constantly rearranging itself like a work of elastic art. And here in Chelm, God had endowed Reb Feibush with that same plasticity. To say that Reb Feibush "knit his brow" would be an understatement, even in a root cellar. When Reb Feibush "raised an eyebrow," one side of his face arranged itself in an upward sweep and the other side became a cascade of falling skin. With so much fluidity on his exterior, how could anyone doubt that there must be something solid happening within Reb Feibush's mind?

Meanwhile, Reb Peretz had buttered the slice of bread he cut, raised it in the air, and dropped it to the floor. Every bit of this he pondered as it happened. The bread fell with the buttered side down. "The answer," observed Reb Peretz, "is definitely in the bread and not in the butter."

Reb Mendel said, "Not so fast! Not so fast." He took another slice of bread, buttered it, and dropped it. This piece fell with the buttered side up. He raised a finger in the air, honored Hillel by standing on one foot, and pronounced a triumphant, "Aha!"

But Reb Feibush narrowed his eyes in thought, which immediately brought the skin of his forehead flowing down over his eyebrows. "This time," he said accusingly to Reb Mendel, "you are only confusing the issue."

Reb Mendel huffed. "Aha," he said, "so you think I am wrong? But here before you is scientific proof! The bread does not always fall with the buttered side down."

Reb Feibush nodded. "To you," he said, "it looks scientific. To Reb Peretz and me, the truth is self-evident. The bread always falls buttered-side down. That is proven. As for why your slice landed buttered-side up, the explanation is equally clear. You buttered your slice of bread on the wrong side!"

Reb Peretz turned to Berel the Dairyman. "Go tell your customers that the sages of the academy have ruled: Your butter is not too heavy. It is the bread that is at fault. Let them blame the baker, not the dairyman."

Happy with his answer, Berel departed, leaving behind a goodly portion of his finest butter.

❁ Another time, a Chelmer asked the sages, "Can you tell me which horse to buy?"

"Of course," said Reb Mendel, "but what are the choices?"

"There is a horse being offered for sale in Zamosc. The owner says that no finer steed can be found anywhere. His horse will pull a cart or carriage, even pull a plow. His horse will eat practically nothing and pay for itself in no time—so the owner says."

"And the other horse?" asked Reb Peretz (even as he had begun to consider what a horse might do to pay for itself).

"The other horse is in Lvov, which is a greater distance. But its owner says that it will do everything the horse from Zamosc will do, and in addition, it is the fastest horse in the region. The owner says that if you set out with this horse from Chelm at three in the morning, you can reach Lublin by six!"

Reb Feibush furrowed his brow, which at the same time furrowed both cheeks. "Which horse is more expensive?"

"That's the rub," said the Chelmer. "Both prices are the same."

Reb Mendel stood on one foot, raised his hand in the air, extended one finger, and said, "Aha!"

Reb Peretz nodded to Reb Mendel and said to the Chelmer, "Reb Mendel reminds me to tell you a story: There was once a donkey that stood in the center of a field. On one side of the field was a delicious-looking haystack. On the other side of the field, there was an equally delicious-looking haystack. The donkey was the same distance from one haystack as he was from the other. He could not make up his mind in which direction to go for his meal. Being a donkey—a stubborn ani-

mal by nature—the donkey starved to death in the center of
the field."

Reb Feibush let the folds of his face fall where they
would. "What Reb Mendel and Reb Peretz are saying is, 'You
should not starve to death while you are trying to decide
which of these two horses to buy.'" To which, he shortly
added, "If you are hungry, we have black bread and some butter that the dairyman left us."

"But which horse should I buy?" the fellow asked.

Reb Peretz said, "That should be obvious. A horse that
can pay for itself is a good investment. As for a horse that can
run fast enough from Chelm at three o'clock in the morning to
reach Lublin by six o'clock in the morning, I ask you, what
can a person do in Lublin at six in the morning?"

❂ Another case involved a young man who aspired to be a
sage. "I will never be a sage," he complained to the three
sages. "Look at me. My chin is bare. My beard will not grow
in. And who has ever heard of a sage without a beard?"

Reb Feibush knitted his famous forehead, tossing his
wrinkles into an asymmetrical pattern that resembled wind-
blown dunes of sand. He asked the youth, "Does your father
have a beard?"

"A full beard," replied the young man.

"Aha!" said Reb Mendel. "Aha!"

Reb Peretz stood and considered Reb Mendel from the tip
of his upraised finger to the toe of the one foot still standing
on the floor. "What Reb Mendel means," he concluded, "is
that your problem is hereditary!"

"But how can that be," asked the young man. "I just told
you that my father has a full beard."

This time, Reb Mendel fairly shouted, "Aha!"

Reb Feibush said, "It's your mother. You inherited your
chin from your mother!"

Reb Peretz prodded, "Unless, that is, your mother has a beard?"

"She has no beard," the youth said thoughtfully. Then he smiled and thanked the sages of the academy of Chelm. "How you have relieved my mind!" he said as he put his hat on his head. "Now I can return to my studies."

❀ One day, no Chelmers came with questions, and there was no meeting of the council of the elders for them to attend. Most of the morning, they sat at the table in silence, until, at last, Reb Peretz of Ponder, for whom silence was nothing more nor less than an opportunity for serious contemplation, turned to his brother sages and said, "I think the time for the *Mashiach* has arrived. The Messiah should be here in Chelm in just a little while."

This eschatological news caused an unexpected furor. Reb Mendel jumped up so quickly he overturned his chair, which fell to the floor with a resounding thud. He raised foot and hand and finger and emitted a series of "Aha's" in a wide variety of inflections.

Reb Feibush's expression changed rapidly in response to each of Reb Mendel's different intonations of "Aha." At one point, he interjected, "Reb Mendel, speak a little slower, please, if you wish me to understand all you are saying." It was to no avail.

Reb Peretz said to Reb Feibush, "Honestly, I have lost the train of this argument. Can you tell me why Reb Mendel is so bothered by the approach of the Messiah?"

Reb Feibush replied, "I will try. First, Reb Mendel notes that Reb Fishel and Minda Leah, the richest people in Chelm, have just built a new house, and if the Messiah is arriving now, they will have no time to enjoy it. Second, he recalls that Saul the Chandler has just repainted the braided candle on the sign over his shop and Velvel the Cobbler has only now replaced the sandal on his door bell with a new boot.

They will reap no benefits in trade from these improvements if the Messiah comes now. Third, he observes, the anticipated feathers have not yet arrived in Chelm, and the elders have as yet found no way to practically dispose of the remaining pearl which would bring wealth to all Chelm, so poverty in Chelm may never disappear if the Messiah appears now."

"He said all that?" asked Reb Peretz.

"More," said Reb Feibush, "but he was speaking so quickly, I could not catch it all."

Reb Mendel picked up his chair, set it beside the table, and resumed his place. Reb Feibush allowed his fingers to thrum the tabletop. Reb Peretz sat lost in thought, pulling nervously on his beard and mumbling to himself. At last, Reb Peretz raised his head. "Tell Reb Mendel not to worry needlessly," he said. "I have considered the matter and this is my opinion:

"In Egypt, our people suffered under the pharaoh. In Persia, the evil Haman tried to put us all to death. Rome tried to crush us, and ever since we have suffered persecution after persecution in the Diaspora. In every instance, God has helped us overcome our troubles. With just a little help from God, we will overcome the Messiah, too!"

❀ Some might believe that the academy of Chelm with its three divisions is an aberration among the great schools of tradition, but the wise know better. The reputation of many of today's foremost scholars rests entirely on brow-knitting as taught by Reb Feibush in the Division of Highbrow Scholarship, even if their faces are not quite as loosely-constructed. At the same time, it is difficult to calculate how many of today's scholars have earned their stature solely through the art of "Aha" as perfected in Reb Mendel's Division of Advanced Amazement. Emulating his delicate balance and the extent of his expressiveness requires a developed degree of nuance. If a scholar places too much emphasis on "Aha," it might lead to the mistaken opinion that he never had an original thought, while placing too little emphasis might be mistaken for plagiarism.

Then, too, many scholars today gain their status by studying the table, examining the ceiling, considering the floor, reflecting on the mirror, cogitating on the carpet, ruminating on whatever food is served them, mulling over their wine, and deliberating on whether or not a book should be closed before going to bed or left open and turned over as if the pages last noticed are too important to be mixed up with the rest of the book. All these arts derive from the academic pursuits inspired by Reb Peretz of Ponder in the Division of Dire Probity.

In short, among the wise men and women of Chelm, the academy of Chelm represents the epitome of what the village is all about.

THE MAYOR'S PRIDE

❀ When Zelig was a little boy, he had a dream. He dreamed he could fly from place to place by jumping into the air and naming the place he wished to go. He flew to towns near Chelm—Brisk and Lublin, Zamosc and Lvov—and then he flew to faraway places. He dreamed he visited Troyes and Vilna, Kiev and Speyer. Just as he was thinking he might visit Jerusalem, he awakened. Climbing out of bed, he was disappointed that he was still as earth-bound as a field mouse. Every night thereafter, as he fell asleep, he tried to bring the same dream. Sometimes he could and sometimes he could not. As he grew older, another thing about the dream intrigued him. Wherever he alighted, whatever place he visited, people admired him and treated him with deference. They bowed to greet him and called him "Reb" Zelig. They stopped and waited for him to pass or stepped aside to make way for him.

Zelig's father was a drayman. As a youth, Zelig was his father's best helper. When he was fourteen, his father said, "Now, you will be a drayman." He purchased for Zelig a new flat wagon and two mighty horses to haul goods from town to town. As he drove his horses, Zelig often wished he could make his trips by flying as he had in his dreams. But no, his real world was hard work; driving being the least of it. There was tending to the horses, caring for the wagon, loading cargo, securing cargo, unloading cargo, and loading cargo again. He envied the merchants whose goods he carried and wished he could own what was on his wagon so he could send someone else off to deliver it.

When Zelig was seventeen, Raisel the Matchmaker found Zelig a suitable bride. The bride price was set and the dowry was paid. Zelig was betrothed to Chasya, the eldest daughter of Velvel the Cobbler. As in small villages everywhere, all Chelm turned out for the wedding, always glad to find a *simcha*, a joyous event, to celebrate. The wedding was memorable for Zelig, too, especially because he fancied the honor people pay the bridegroom on his wedding day. He loved being lifted high in a chair by dancing Chelmers who paraded him around the hall. He did not mind that equal or more attention was being paid to the bride, or that she, too, was being lifted and paraded. He found Chasya very comely, as girls from Chelm tend to be, and he liked her father Velvel.

Zelig and Chasya soon had their first child, a boy they called Tzvi Selig. Becoming a father also brought Zelig into the limelight. He thoroughly enjoyed the attention he got just because he had a newborn son.

One night, soon after Tzvi Selig was born, Zelig told Chasya about his dream and about how he felt when people paid attention to him, gave him respect, and honored him. Chasya heard his yearning, comforted him, and said, "I think the time will come." Zelig often thought of Chasya's words as he brushed the horses or drove the cart.

Time passed. Tzvi Selig was joined by a little sister, Miriam Mindl. Zelig's father passed away, followed by his mother. Zelig hired out his father's dray and its two draft horses. In a year or two, he bought a third team and a third wagon and hired that one out, too. He still drove his dray, but now he took less trips and trips closer to home. Zelig and Chasya built a new house closer to the town center. For a Chelmer, Zelig made a nice living. He was invited to join the council of elders. Chasya said, "The time has come." Zelig was not sure. He was still a drayman and a father and people liked him, but they did not esteem him.

Then Chelm's mayor resigned and the hunt for a new mayor began. Zelig thought, "That's what I am seeking."

Meanwhile, up on The Hill, Minda Leah said to her husband, Reb Fishel, "You are the richest man in town, but you get no reward for all you do! You should become the mayor of Chelm. Who is better fit for the job?"

"And what makes me fit to be mayor?" Reb Fishel asked.

"Remember the gold coins you gave when the people wanted to buy justice? Your generosity makes you fit. And how do these people of Chelm show their gratitude? They should make you their mayor."

"I do not even attend meetings," said Reb Fishel. "I am nervous whenever I have to speak in public. I could never come right out and say, 'I am the richest man in town. I own the lumber mill. I should be mayor.'"

Minda Leah said, "No. That would never do. Asking to be mayor because you are rich would only offend the elders. But I have a plan. Do as I tell you and they will make you mayor. From now on, you will attend the meetings of the elders and no matter what they say to you, you will stand and reply, 'I will have none of that!' Then they will see that you know what you want and they will respect you."

"That's all? Just say, 'I will have none of that!'?"

"Believe me, you will soon have them eating out of your hand."

At the very next meeting of the elders, everyone was surprised to see Reb Fishel in attendance.

Yankel the Tailor stood. "Let us welcome Reb Fishel," he said. "We are honored that he has decided to come to the meeting of our council."

Naftali the Water Carrier stood. "Let us make Reb Fishel a member of our council."

The other elders nodded their heads and complimented Naftali on his excellent suggestion. So Naftali turned to Reb Fishel and motioned. "Reb Fishel, come take a seat on the council of the elders of the village of Chelm."

Reb Fishel stood and said, "I will have none of that!"

The elders were stunned. Reb Feivel, the Glory of Chelm and its rabbi, tried to blunt the blow by saying: "Reb Fishel is obviously like Moses, a man of humility; such a man should not be coerced into becoming an elder."

At this explanation, there was a sigh of relief. The elders went back to their business. The question for the day was how to pay for a new roof for the synagogue. Zev the Treasurer reminded everyone that the town treasury was at its normal level. Drained.

Naftali the Water Carrier said, "Since it is the roof of the synagogue, all Chelmers should be concerned. Let us agree that everyone in Chelm will pay a fair share."

Suddenly, Reb Fishel stood and pounded one fist into his other hand. "I will have none of that!" he barked.

The elders sat back, surprised. Reb Fishel had never been known to be so demonstrative. Zev the Treasurer smiled and said, "Reb Fishel, if you insist on paying for the entire synagogue roof, so be it. We will not refuse your generous offer."

Raisel the Matchmaker said, "Such a gesture! Reb Fishel, your name will be known throughout Chelm."

Reb Fishel pounded the other fist into the other hand. "I will have none of that!" he boomed.

Tzeitel the Butcher's Wife said, "So you wish your gift to be anonymous? Such charity! Such humility! Everyone will want to be your friend!"

Reb Fishel sat down. But when he saw that all eyes were turned to him, he stood again, and with a little less certainty than before, he said, "I will have none of that!"

The meeting soon ended and Reb Fishel went home to his wife. Minda Leah asked, "Did you do as I instructed? Did you let them know that you are not a pushover?"

"I did what you said, but it was very confusing. I think I agreed to pay for a new roof for the synagogue."

"But you were only supposed to say, 'I will have none of that!'"

"I promise you, Minda Leah, those were the only words I uttered."

"Never mind," said Minda Leah. "My plan will still work. I will take the next step."

Minda Leah dressed in her finest outfit and walked down to Sissel's café in the heart of Chelm. Sissel was a town elder and Minda Leah knew that what she said to Sissel would be repeated to all the elders. Trying to appear casual, she began, "I hear that my husband, Reb Fishel, was at the meeting of the elders today. He knows how to stand up for himself, don't you agree?"

Sissel was pouring coffee into Minda Leah's cup. "It is certain that he stood up. He offered to pay for the new roof of the synagogue. He refused to be on the council of the elders. And he insisted that he needs no new friends."

Minda Leah winked at Sissel, "Perhaps he was hoping for a position more exalted than elder?"

Sissel looked thoughtful. "Well, we do need a new mayor. I'll discuss it with the elders."

"There is no rush," said Minda Leah. "I'll bring Reb Fishel to the meeting of the elders tomorrow morning."

That night, Minda Leah bragged to Reb Fishel that her plan was working! He would surely be the next mayor of Chelm, she said, and she congratulated herself over and over. But Minda Leah's plan had one flaw.

The next morning, Minda Leah brought Reb Fishel to the meeting of the council. Zev the Treasurer rose and said, "I nominate Reb Fishel for mayor of Chelm."

Minda Leah pushed Reb Fishel to his feet. This was the big moment. "Talk!" she whispered to him.

Reb Fishel said, "I will have none of that!"

Minda Leah stepped on his foot and punched him in the ribs with her finger. In response, Reb Fishel thundered, "I will have none of that!"

And thus was crushed the well-laid plan of Minda Leah.

❀ Before long, Zelig was elected mayor of Chelm. A month went by, and one night he said to Chasya, "It's not working."

"Why not? You are the mayor of Chelm. Isn't that what you wanted?"

"I am the mayor, but people see me and ignore me as they always did. If only I had a uniform, then they would know I was mayor."

"Do mayors wear uniforms?" asked Chasya.

"In Lvov, the mayor wears a red satin sash so everyone knows he is mayor. In Zamosc, the mayor wears a hat with a pheasant feather so everyone knows he is mayor."

Chasya suggested, "Rely on the pride of Chelm's elders. Tell them how the other mayors wear costumes and they will want to make an outfit for you."

The elders met soon thereafter and Zelig raised the issue of a uniform for the mayor. Kalman the Fixer immediately took up the cudgel. "If other towns make special clothing for their mayors, Chelm should, too. Perhaps we should make a red satin sash for Zelig."

Zalman Shelomo objected. "If people see the red satin sash, they will mistake Zelig for the mayor of Lvov."

"And if they see a pheasant feather on his hat," said Tzeitel, "they will think the mayor of Zamosc is visiting Chelm."

Consideration turned on lace collars, epaulets, gold buttons, striped pants, a belled vest, and red stockings. None seemed quite right as a mayor's attire. So the council sent out for food and began to seek something gaudy but more dignified. After lunch, the thought of satin underwear was dismissed, and the practicality of a cape was seriously questioned in light of the rainy season which was due at any moment.

Yankel the Tailor rose. "Zelig's father-in-law is Velvel the Cobbler. Why not ask Velvel to fashion a special pair of shoes for our new mayor?"

The elders applauded this suggestion. Shoes seemed a fitting costume. After a little more discourse, Reb Feibush of the academy of Chelm was assigned to speak with Velvel the Cobbler whose shop was located right beside the academy.

A week passed and Velvel delivered the shoes to the elders. The elders were delighted, and as soon as Zelig saw them, he, too, was pleased. Surely, there was not another pair of shoes like these anywhere. They were light as sponge cake and of the same golden color. And the laces were woven of white thread twisted with gold braid. Surely, Chelm would be proud of a mayor who wore golden shoes! Zelig slipped them on at once. Could there be any doubt? They were a perfect fit! (Well, obviously, this was not the first pair of shoes that Velvel had made for his son-in-law.)

The elders passed a law: "No one in Chelm is permitted to wear golden slippers except the mayor."

Just as the vote was taken and the law officially went into effect, there came a clap of thunder and a bolt of lightning that signaled the opening of the skies and the first rain of the season.

The next day, Zelig stood before the elders, and in a disappointed tone, said, "The wisdom of Chelm leaves much to be desired. Look at how useless are the golden slippers you have chosen as your mayor's uniform!" He took off one shoe and held it on high. It was anything but golden. The lovely slipper was caked with mud.

"The rains always turn the streets to a muddy mess," said Tzeitel. "There is no wisdom that can overcome that."

"But as long as it is muddy," said Zelig, "the golden slippers are no sign that can be identified. I cannot be recognized in them!"

Reb Peretz of Ponder was mulling over the problem. "I think I have a solution. Let me talk with Velvel the Cobbler. Give us a day or two, and perhaps all will be well."

Now, it is not called "the rainy season" by mistake. No, the rain kept falling steadily for the next two days. The streets had been muddy; now even the wooden sidewalks were slippery with a thin coat of mud.

Nevertheless, Velvel delivered his new solution for Zelig's problem. The elders approved by their clapping. Velvel had fashioned a pair of boots that could be slipped over the golden slippers to protect them! Velvel cleaned and polished the slippers until they shone as they had when they were new. Then Velvel slid them one by one onto Zelig's feet, and over each slipper he put a new leather boot to protect it from the mud.

The next day, Zelig again stood before the elders and complained. "The boots are no answer. They protect the slippers, but they also keep the slippers from being seen. As I walk through the town, no one knows that I am the mayor. I may as well resign."

Reb Feivel, the Glory of Chelm, rose to respond. "This is nothing more than a test of our wisdom. Surely, there is a way that the boots can protect the slippers and yet the golden slippers can be seen. Some kind of window...."

Reb Mendel of Apt jumped to his feet. He raised a finger in the air, stood on one foot in honor of the great sage Hillel, and emitted a sharp, "Aha!"

Reb Feibush of Lublin raised one eyebrow, throwing the skin on that side of his face up into a miniature peak while simultaneously forming a canyon of flesh on the opposite side. "Reb Mendel tells us that windows will not do, but he suggests that placing holes strategically in the boots will make the golden slippers visible when Zelig walks."

So the boots were returned to Velvel the Cobbler who cut holes in the top of each and small openings on the side of each. Velvel did not wait for the next meeting of the council of elders. He was happy for any reason to visit his daughter Chasya, his grandson Tzvi Selig, and his granddaughter Miriam Mindl. He delivered the holey boots in person to Zelig. The evening was convivial. They shared tea and schnapps and some of Chasya's fine cookies.

But the next morning, an unhappy Zelig again rose before the council of elders. "The boots with the holes are not the answer, either. As you can see, I wore them only this morning with the following result: the boots get muddy, the holes fill with mud, and all that can be seen of the golden slippers is mud."

Sissel stood and offered her opinion. "The trouble is," she said, "people grow from the ground up instead of from the top down. If people grew from the top down, Zelig could just keep his feet above the ground during the rainy season."

There was a thoughtful pause as if the elders were actually wondering how to make use of Sissel's thought. Then Zev the Treasurer spoke to break the spell, "We thank Sissel for her little insight. My dear colleagues, think! There must be wisdom in Chelm that will solve the problem. How can we ensure that the golden shoes be seen by all?"

Kalman the Fixer rose next. "Perhaps we should stuff straw into the holes of the boots to protect the golden shoes from the mud."

Tzeitel the Butcher's Wife said, "The straw will just get muddy, and even if it did not, it would prevent the golden slippers from showing through."

In an impasse like this, all eyes turned to the rabbi. Unfortunately, he was napping. Yankel shook him and filled him in on the current state of affairs. Reb Feivel, the Glory of Chelm, yawned. Then he rose to his full height.

"If the golden slippers cannot be seen on Zelig the Mayor's feet because of the mud," Reb Feivel said, "then let Zelig wear the golden slippers on his hands. All in Chelm will see the shoes, know who Zelig is, and pay him the respect due the mayor of the village of Chelm."

The elders all agreed. If he had not already been called the Glory of Chelm, the rabbi would have earned his title that day.

As the rabbi advised, Zelig wore the shoes on his hands for a whole month, during which Chelmers who saw him recognized him as the mayor, bowed when he came nigh, and stepped aside to make way for the man with the golden slippers. The elders were happy. And Zelig was happy with the recognition and deference he so coveted. Chasya had been right: his time had come.

But Chasya had a better idea still—after all, she was the daughter of a cobbler! She took a length of leather strap, and in her father's shop she fashioned a harness for Zelig the Drayman. On each side of the harness in front, she attached one golden slipper. In this way, Zelig's hands were free to salute every Chelmer who saluted him, and Zelig could take a drink in the tavern without taking off his slippers. And that is how the mayor of Chelm acquired his well-deserved cognomen, Zelig the Bedecked.

THE MONUMENT

❀ Sometimes the superior wisdom of the elders of the village of Chelm led to results that were, unfortunately, far ahead of their time. This was the case when, for example, the elders sought to create a monument atop Chelm's mountain. The debate regarding what kind of marker would best express the pride of Chelm was far-ranging.

The suggestion that an enormous plum be constructed—in honor of the foremost product of Chelm which was yearly harvested for fine jam, preserves, and schnapps—was quashed only because an iconic metal plum was already suspended from the noose on the miniature gallows which formed the "spire" of the new Town Hall.

The suggestion that a giant statue of Grandfather Pike—the elusive fish that inhabited Chelm's river and had outwitted the finest efforts of Chelm's shrewd fishermen, proving wilier and more slippery at every turn—was defeated when Dovidl the Nose stated flatly that it was only a matter of time before Grandfather Pike would grace the Sabbath table in some rich Chelmer's home. Fish can be sneaky for many years, but eventually, as it is the destiny of every Chelmer to be wise, it is the destiny of every fish to be netted. Dovidl the Nose refused to budge from this stance even when a salient objection was raised to point out that Grandfather Pike was both a fish and a Chelmer! He rebutted the argument deftly by inquiring, "How would it feel if the symbol of Chelm was one day fried in a pan?"

Reb Feivel's suggestion that an enormous Eternal Light should be constructed at the top of the mountain was considered from several points of view. While the elders generally liked the notion that Chelm was eternal and should be represented by a flame that was eternal, some worried that the breeze might carry the flames from a gigantic Eternal Light into the groves of poplar and pine, setting fire to the trees. Even if this could be avoided, Hirschel the Wood Carrier argued, the fire would require that trees be consumed on a daily basis so that it would tax the best efforts of a number of woodsmen to supply the fuel for the light, and that, as trees close to the flame were depleted, the woodsmen would have to range farther and farther from the Eternal Light to keep it supplied, which, in turn, would require the best efforts of a goodly number of wood carriers. But the ultimate argument against an Eternal Light being the symbol of Chelm was brought forward by Zelig the Bedecked, the mayor of Chelm, who recalled the mud which some years before had so bedeviled him and prevented him from wearing his golden slippers on his feet and had relegated the precious shoes to the harness that now decorated his chest and shoulders, for Zelig reminded the elders that Chelm's rainy season was like Chelm itself, entirely inevitable. No Eternal Flame could possibly weather the rains.

The suggestion that a giant pearl be constructed and placed at the top of the hill was defeated because Zev the Treasurer objected that calling attention to the single precious pearl in Chelm's treasury might only serve to attract a number of unwanted characters to the village. Chelm should be satisfied with its one resident thief, the shrewd Gedaliah the Goniff, Zev argued, and not purposely seek to import more of his kind. But the defeat of the Enormous Pearl Plan brought in its wake the suggestion that the new monument to Chelm should be a giant feather. After all, as Hirschel pointed out, the feathers of Chelm were still blowing in the wind and would soon make their way triumphantly home the way a horse that strays will eventually follow its instinct for food and make its way to its owner's doorstep. Sissel's piercing logic ended the campaign for the giant feather for, as she pointed out, "Where would we find a bird gargantuan enough for one of its feathers, even a tail feather, to be seen from the top of the mountain?"

Ostentatiously imbibing in a pinch of snuff and giving a manly sneeze into his handkerchief, Zelig the Bedecked, the mayor of Chelm, remarked that many towns and villages honored their prominent citizens with finely-carved statues. Perhaps a statue of the mayor of Chelm should be set up at the top of the mountain? Yankel the Tailor wove a virtual spider's web around the mayor's suggestion by saying, "Of course, dear Mayor, you are aware that towns and villages do this for mayors and other leading citizens who are dead? Do you propose that we should postpone this discussion until you pass on and then consider the matter in your absence?" Zelig the Bedecked sneezed again into his handkerchief. Without further comment, the elders passed on to the next suggestion.

"Perhaps," began Tzeitel the Butcher's Wife, "we should consider making a monument of something distinctive, something impressive, and something which Chelm does not already possess?"

"Yes," said Sissel, the owner of the café. "I remember that our mayor once suggested constructing the name of the town in giant letters at the top of the hill, a sign to read "CHELM" so people looking up would know they are in Chelm."

"But what if the wind, which is stronger at the top of the mountain than it is here in the village, knocked over one letter?" inquired Kalman. "Then we would be living in a different town altogether!"

Reb Peretz of Ponder stood. "If we think this through to its end," he declared, "we will realize that there is at least one thing which Chelm does not possess that is possessed by Brisk, Lvov, Lublin, and Tishevitz."

"Is this a riddle," asked Raisel the Matchmaker, "or do you know the answer?"

"The answer is always in the question," said Reb Feibush of Lublin, wrinkling his brow in the extraordinary way he had of wrinkling his entire face. "In this case, the answer is 'a bridge.'"

As if to place an exclamation point on the fine wisdom of Reb Peretz and Reb Feibush, the third sage of the academy of Chelm, Reb Mendel of Apt, shot to his feet, raised one foot off the ground in the manner of Hillel, pointed a finger Heavenward, and cried out, "A-HA!" placing all his considerable emphasis on the "ha!"

The council of the elders of the village of Chelm voted, and it was decreed that a bridge should be built at the top of the mountain. They assigned Kalman the Fixer, who had done such a splendid job on Chelm's last building project, to construct the bridge. "And remember," Zelig the Bedecked, mayor of Chelm said, "it must be monumental."

So the work began. The first difficulty arose while digging holes for the footings of the bridge. The diggers suddenly stopped (actually, as soon as their spades touched the earth for the first time). They huddled together, speaking to one another in low tones. Then one of the diggers approached Kalman the Fixer, who was sitting alone, drawing the bridge in his imagination so he would know what it should look like.

The digger stood above Kalman and said, "There is a serious problem. If we dig the holes, where will we put the dirt that we dig up?"

Kalman the Fixer knew that for every problem there is a fix, if only you can imagine it. Then, as in so many other cases in his history of patching and restoring, the answer came in a flash. He pointed to an open spot just below the top of the mountain where no trees happened to be growing. "There," he said to the digger, "that is the right place. Dig a big hole there and put all the dirt from the holes you dig at the top of the mountain into the hole there."

So all the diggers left the top of the mountain and went to the spot Kalman had indicated and dug a big hole there. Soon the digger who had come to Kalman before, approached him again. "There is a serious problem," he said. "We have to know what to do with the dirt that was left over from the big hole we made to hold the dirt from the holes that we are about to make for the footings of the bridge."

Kalman looked around. He spied a larger opening in the trees, pointed to it, and said, "Look there, I think you can dig a new hole over there that will be large enough for all the dirt you have just dug up and also for all the dirt that you will dig up to make the new hole."

So all the diggers went to the new spot Kalman had designated and dug an enormous hole. But soon the lone digger approached Kalman again. "There is still a problem," he said. "A great pile of dirt is left over from the enormous hole that we made to hold the dirt from the big hole that we dug to hold the dirt leftover from the footings of the bridge that we are about to dig. What do we do with the new pile of dirt?"

Kalman the Fixer did not hesitate a moment. The answer was his in a jiffy. "Take the leftover dirt from the enormous hole and pile it on the very top of the mountain. That will make the mountain taller so that when we finish the bridge it will sit even higher and be seen from an even greater distance."

Proud of himself, Kalman the Fixer watched as the diggers shoveled the huge pile of dirt into sacks, tamped down the sacks, carried the sacks of dirt up the mountain, and dumped sack after sack of dirt on the mountaintop. When this was done, the diggers dug the holes for the footings of the bridge, carting the dirt from the holes of the bridge footings to the big hole they had prepared for it in the opening Kalman had first pointed out. When there was more dirt than they could fit in the big hole, they packed it into sacks, took it back up to the top of the mountain and—being careful not to fill in the holes for the footings of the bridge—they dumped the extra dirt on top to make the mountain higher still.

Since the bridge was to be made of stone, the diggers now became stone carriers. Of course, there was no stone at the top of the mountain. But over the years, stone had broken off through natural erosion and fallen down the mountain, so there were piles of good stone all around the mountain's foot. The task was to bring these stones back up to the top. Kalman was disappointed at first. It took five men half a day to bring five stones from the bottom to the top of the mountain. But Kalman was not called "the fixer" for nothing! He had a brilliant idea, which he shared with the men at the top.

"Instead of carrying the stones up one by one," he told them, "you can load five or six stones into a barrow and push them up the mountain."

Since the mountain of Chelm was really a hill, and the slope of the hillside was not all that severe, the men immediately saw the sense in Kalman's plan. So they carried the five stones they had brought up one by one down the mountain, loaded them into a wheelbarrow, and pushed them back up the mountain in no time. Then they emptied the barrow and went back down the mountain for more stones.

When Kalman thought that enough stones had been gathered at the top of the mountain, the men who had been diggers and then stone carriers became water carriers, bringing pails of water up from the river. They crushed some of the softer stones and mixed them with water, sand, and lime to make a mortar paste. Then the water carriers became stone masons.

The work went on for months. Every new problem, Kalman the Fixer solved with his undaunted creativity. The elders looked up daily to see the structure taking shape.

The stones were cleverly fitted to make a broad arch with a carved keystone to hold it in place and give strength to the platform above. How impressive it looked when the morning sun peeked through the bottom of the arch and then lit the bridge from behind and then rose above the bridge like a beacon! Everyone in Chelm was caught up in admiration for this new monument to the wisdom of Chelm.

When the work was complete, there was a party at the top of the mountain and all Chelm turned out. Children ran across the bridge. Couples stood at the center of the bridge and looked down at the houses on the shelf of the mountain called The Hill (where only the wealthy usually looked down) and at the village and its wall down below. Picnics were spread around the bridge, under the bridge, and even on the bridge's wooden platform.

"We should build a statue of Kalman the Fixer, our own master builder," said Raisel the Matchmaker, delighted with the bridge and delighted with the party.

Zelig the Bedecked, the mayor of Chelm, gave a "harrumph" from deep in his throat and replied to Raisel, "We should wait until he's dead and gone." Then he added, "He should only live so long!"

The rejoicing over the bridge lasted for many a day.

Yet, somewhere in the Holy Books it is written, "Pride goeth before a fall." That fall, in fact, arrived with a vengeance. The autumn rains slowly turned the loose dirt that the diggers had poured on top of the mountain—to raise the top of the mountain, to make the bridge higher than it would otherwise have been—to Chelm's nemesis, mud. And the mud commenced to slide. This might not have been so egregious except that the holes for the footings had been dug in the loose dirt that had formed the new top of the mountain, so the footings began to slide with the mud.

It could have been worse. When the bridge's arch lost support and the keystone gave way, the whole stone bridge might have toppled down on the town of Chelm. In this instance, however, the rains ate away at the bridge little by little so that the stones fell from its center outward. The mud and stones may have considered tumbling down on Chelm, but surely the Holy One intervened. The mud slid sideways and the whole structure—mortar, stone, and wood—slid with it, crashing down the mountain and into the river.

In the meantime, as the rain fell, many people of Chelm noticed what was happening up above and ran to the synagogue to recite the Book of Psalms, which, as everyone knows, is the surest way to avert imminent disaster. Others had no idea that the bridge was falling and heard no distinctive crash when it fell since thunder from the heavens accompanied the storm. Some of the elders realized the danger before the crash, some were reciting Psalms, some heard the crash, and some were standing aghast in the rain.

Kalman the Fixer was in the synagogue sitting in the back near the door. His head was in his hands, and he was weeping bitterly. The rabbi, Reb Feivel, the Glory of Chelm, came and sat by his side. He took one of Kalman's hands in his and said, "Be comforted, my friend. No one will blame you. After all, the Tower of Babel must have been a mighty sight before Heaven tore it down. So you built a beautiful bridge and everyone loved it. They will remember that." And he added, almost beneath his breath, "It's just that Heaven probably would have been happier with an Eternal Light."

At the next meeting of the council of the elders of the village of Chelm, it was decided that there should be no blame placed for the collapse of the bridge. As Hirschel explained, there never was any practical reason for a bridge to be built at the top of a mountain, anyway. After days of discussion, it was decided that something practical should replace the bridge, something the town could see as a monument, but actually put to use. So the elders called for food and resumed the issue of what to build, which after seven days and seven nights, they settled.

The elders decided to build a proper watermill for Chelm at the top of the mountain—a watermill to grind grain with proper grindstones to be ordered from Lublin and with a giant waterwheel to turn the grindstones. This decision was duly recorded in the town records, and should the treasury of

Chelm ever be able to afford it, a watermill will one day stand as a practical replacement for the bridge that was atop the mountain.

THE NIGHT WATCHMAN

✹ Once a year, the fishermen of Brisk challenged the fishermen of Zamosc to a race to see whose team could row the fastest from Brisk to Zamosc. The river connecting Brisk and Zamosc ran beside Chelm. In fact, the Chelmers called it the Chelm River, and they thought of the fishermen of Chelm as the wisest fishermen along the river.

Still, Chelm's fishermen did not take part in the race. An old tale, probably fabricated, told how once the fishermen of Chelm were challenged to a race against the fishermen of Zamosc. They practiced and practiced, but on the day of the race, when the boat from Zamosc crossed the finish line, the boat from Chelm was far behind. Chelm had lost the race so badly that it was certain something major had gone awry. The elders met and decided to challenge Zamosc again, but before that, they sent Havel, the son of Shmul the Fishmonger, to spy on the racing team from Zamosc as they practiced. When Havel returned, he reported that Chelm could never win against Zamosc unless the Chelm fishermen made drastic changes to their technique.

"What kind of changes?" asked Moishe the Elder, who was in charge of Chelm's seven man racing team.

"For one thing," answered Havel, "the Zamosc team uses its seven men in exactly the opposite way we use ours; they have six fishermen rowing and only one fisherman yelling, 'Faster! Faster!'"

The more likely reason that Chelm's fishermen never participated in the annual race was because Chelm employed small, wide rowboats while the rowboats of Zamosc and Brisk were larger, more streamlined, and faster on the water. The Chelm fishermen seldom found it necessary to range far from Chelm except when they were on barges taking cargo up or down the river. Now, if there had been a barge race....

Despite the fact that Chelm was not entered, the race was a happening, and Chelmers love an occasion, so they turned out. They gathered on the docks, sat on the mountainside, and perched along the top of Chelm's wall. This beautiful spring day, in fact, there were crowds all along the river from Zamosc to Brisk. And wherever there are crowds, there are pickpockets. Who knows how many pickpockets worked the crowds in Zamosc and Brisk? In Chelm, though, there was only one sly thief.

In the Holy Books, it is written, "Poverty pursues the poor." In Chelm, it was Gedaliah the Goniff doing the pursuing—and rich or poor, poverty followed in his wake. His hands were fast, his feet danced, and his body was lithe and quick.

As the rowboats with their teams of oarsmen came down the river, everyone's attention was riveted on the race. In the front of the boats, a fisherman sat beating a drum. In the back, a fisherman worked the tiller. In between, three fishermen on each side rowed, propelling the rowboats forward to the drummer's rhythm. On the down beat, all the fishermen sang out, "Ho!" On the upbeat, they all shouted, "Hey!"

In the excitement, Chelmers in the crowd paid little heed to jostling and touching. Gedaliah's hands flashed and flitted. The boats raced by to the beat of "Ho! Hey! Ho! Hey!" Gedaliah weaseled through the throng, hands gliding from pocket to pocket. As the boats passed Chelm, Gedaliah was about to pick one more pocket when he glanced up and saw Zalman Shelomo standing before him.

"*Shalom aleichem*, greetings to you, my friend the gatekeeper," said Gedaliah the Goniff, stuffing his hands into his own pockets. "How goes it with you on this lovely spring day?"

"*Aleichem shalom*, greetings to you in return," said Zalman Shelomo. "I trust you are behaving yourself today?"

"I am doing my best," said Gedaliah.

"See that you do not do your worst," said Zalman Shelomo, watching carefully as Gedaliah the Goniff backed away and slipped off into the village. Zalman Shelomo thought, "Ah, if only there were three of me, I would arrest that goniff and make sure he was brought to justice. But, as there is still only one of me, there is not much I can do."

The next morning, the council of the elders of Chelm met in the new Town Hall. Before Zelig the Bedecked, the mayor of Chelm, had a chance to call the meeting to order, dozens of Chelmers were crowding the hall and grumbling all at once.

"A pox on thieves! My pocket was picked during the race. How will I buy fish for the Sabbath?"

"The coins I had in my apron are gone—may the filthy goniff who stole them wake up dead! I don't even know when it happened!"

"My purse was taken right off my belt. May the locusts of Egypt consume that loathsome thief!"

The complaints came from every quarter—the widow Ditza; the orphan Isaac; Froyim, the rich hemp merchant; even Heschy, Chelm's professional beggar—all had been victimized as the boats glided past.

Zalman Shelomo the Gatekeeper, the closest thing Chelm had to a policeman, raised his considerable bulk and motioned for silence. "I know that goniff, Gedaliah, is to blame. When I found him in the crowd, I chased him away."

Baruch the Tobacconist stepped forward. "If Gedaliah the Goniff can do this in the daytime—by the light of the sun—imagine what he can do in darkness! He could steal my best pipes, snatch my tobacco, and grab my snuff while I am sleeping."

"He could steal my grain," said Yudel. "What would I have left to sell? He might even filch my scale!"

"He could help himself to my hemp!" cried Froyim. "Who can rest with that goniff on the loose?"

Little by little, panic spread through the room. Every merchant worried about his goods, his shop, and his livelihood. As long as Gedaliah the Goniff was at large, everything they owned was at risk. In their imaginations, they prophesied that soon nothing of Chelm would be left untouched.

The elders debated for a while. They were about to send out for food when Yankel the Tailor had an idea. "We feel safe in the daytime because we are in our shops, watching. It's only the nighttime that spells danger. What if we close our stores and shops and stalls during the day and stay awake through the nights, watching?"

Instead of sending for food, the elders adopted the Chelm Nighttime Plan, convinced it would keep the shops safe. For several days, the shopkeepers closed their concerns during the daylight hours and opened at night, staying open until dawn. Now, it was true that while the Nighttime Plan was in effect, Gedaliah the Goniff did not rob a single shop, but the shopkeepers also made no sales, and their wives and children complained they were away when they should be home (with many a wife adding that her husband was home when he should be away, a fact not more comforting to her).

The third morning, the rabbi sent the shammes from house to house to bang on each shopkeeper's door and summon them to the new Town Hall. They came yawning, stretching, rubbing the sleep from their eyes. The elders were ready to meet them. The rabbi, Reb Feivel, stood and spoke.

"The Chelm Nighttime Plan for protecting the shops is turning Chelm into a Godless place," announced Reb Feivel, the Glory of Chelm. "Before, if only nine people came to the synagogue in the morning to pray, the shammes went out into the street to enlist one more Chelmer to make the *min-yan* of ten men required to begin the prayers. Now, ten men cannot be found, even in the street—much less in the synagogue! And this is true not only for the morning service, when we should thank God for awakening us, but also for the afternoon service, when we should thank God for making our day successful."

"Rabbi," said Baruch the Tobacconist, "the Nighttime Plan is no blessing for us, either. No one comes to buy snuff in the middle of the night. No one shops for candles or spools of thread or fresh vegetables from the carts."

"We must open our shops in the daytime, as always," declared Velvel the Cobbler, "and we must do it soon, or else we and our families will starve."

So the council of the elders of Chelm endeavored to find a new way to guard the shops from Gedaliah the Goniff, a way that would allow the shopkeepers to sleep at night. Ah, the wisdom of Chelm! Again, the answer presented itself even before it became necessary for the elders to send for a meal.

"It is well-known," said Zalman Shelomo the Gatekeeper, "that if there were three of me, we would already have brought that impious wretch Gedaliah the Goniff to justice. Nu, we know that Chelm cannot afford three of me." (So many Chelmers smiled and nodded at this bulky thought that the room itself seemed to bob up and down.)

Reb Mendel of Apt jumped up, stood on one foot in the style of Hillel of beloved memory, raised a hand in the air, and stretched out a finger, saying, "Aha!"

Reb Peretz of Ponder left off gazing at the floor and spoke off-handedly, "You all know what Reb Mendel means. He suggests we should hire a night watchman."

"That was what I meant, too," said Zalman Shelomo. "Then at least there would be two of me."

Zelig the Bedecked, the mayor of Chelm, asked the obvious question, "Where will we find a night watchman? It would have to be someone who has no shop and no occupation."

"It's a match! We have such a one!" exclaimed Raisel the Matchmaker. "Let us hire Heschy the Village Beggar!"

The sound of approbation was immediate. It may be that Heschy seemed even more acceptable because he was not present to speak for himself. In any case, he was duly nominated and elected to be Chelm's new night watchman. Zalman Shelomo was sent to inform him of the Night Watchman Plan, to instruct him on his new job, and to assure him that the shopkeepers would pay him each morning for the work he did the night before.

At first Heschy was opposed. "I already work," he told Zalman Shelomo. "All day I plead, cajole, beseech, entreat, and supplicate. Begging is no easy way to make a living, I assure you."

"If so, it will be more restful for you to be the night watchman," Zalman Shelomo responded. "All you need to do is walk about the town square and keep an eye peeled. If you see a thief, you alert the shopkeepers. The point is, the thief will know you are watching, so he will not rob by night. And you will be paid every morning without begging."

"It still sounds like work," said Heschy suspiciously.

"Try it," said Zalman Shelomo.

For many nights, Heschy stayed awake, meandering around, ensuring the shops were dark and safe. Every morning, he received his pay. Every day, he slept. He was beginning to like being Chelm's night watchman. And the shopkeepers and merchants of Chelm were happy, too.

This satisfying interlude came to an end when the rains returned to Chelm and the wind blew chill. Heschy complained to the elders, "Do you think that a night watchman can patrol at night when he is shivering? What if I catch cold? A cold can be dangerous. It can turn to pneumonia, and from pneumonia I could die. Could I patrol the town after I am dead?"

The elders considered the difficulty. In the end, they decided it would be reasonable to buy Heschy a fur coat. But

Minda Leah heard what the elders had decided, and she came to the next meeting to complain.

"As everyone knows," began Minda Leah, "my husband, Reb Fishel, is the richest man in Chelm. And people know him in the winter by the fur coat he wears. What kind of respect are you giving to Reb Fishel if you allow the former beggar to wear a fur coat?"

Yankel the Tailor said, "To this, I have an answer. Reb Fishel's fur coat is made like all fine coats with the fur on the outside. I can make a fur coat for our night watchman inside-out, with the skin on the outside and the fur on the inside!"

Again, the plan was adopted before there was time to send for food. So much fast thinking was almost unheard of in Chelm. It began to worry Sissel, the owner of Chelm's café, for it threatened her very livelihood. She could only pray in silence that the elders would continue to be brilliant, but at a slower pace.

Her prayers were instantly answered. Heschy the Night Watchman objected to the fur coat. "Do you want to kill me?" he asked. "Wearing a fur coat at night could attract wolves the way blossoms attract bees. Wolves could mistake me for a wild animal and attack me in a pack. If I am lying ripped to shreds in the night, who will protect the shops from the goniff?"

Now, the elders sent out for food, upon which Sissel gave inward thanks to the Holy One who looks after us. Much discussion was necessary to solve this new dilemma. Many hours later, Kalman the Fixer proposed that a horse be bought for Heschy the Night Watchman so that he could ride on his rounds through the town and not be afraid of being attacked by wolves.

Just as this proposal was about to be approved, Heschy objected. "What kind of Chelmer rides a horse on its back? Do I look like somebody who can control a horse from on top? And if I fall, I am sure to break my neck, if not a shoulder or arm.

What good will I be lying broken instead of riding like some crazy cavalryman?"

Zev the Treasurer was the first to answer. "In the middle of the town square, beside the well, there is a hitching post. If Heschy sits on the horse and the horse is tied to the post, he will be tall enough to see all around. He can be the night watchman, looking out for thieves, protected from the cold by his fur coat, protected from the wolves by the horse, and protected from falling by not having to move the horse."

There was genuine applause. Even Heschy had no further complaint to raise. The inside-out coat was fashioned by Yankel the Tailor. The horse was rented from the stable of Zelig the Bedecked. As night approached, the horse was tied to the post in the midst of the town square beside the well. A small chair helped Heschy climb aboard the horse. What a fine figure was cut by the mounted night watchman! Surely, the wisdom of Chelm had prevailed.

Two nights passed without event. On the third morning, Heschy the Night Watchman ran into the synagogue before the morning prayers began and cried out, "Shopkeepers! Hurry to your stores! The thieves were busy last night!"

The shopkeepers in the synagogue were shocked, and they ran from the synagogue, yelling "Thief! Thief!" all the way to their shops. Their cries alerted those who were not in the synagogue to come running to their stores and stalls. Many a shop had an empty shelf here and there; stalls had a missing barrel of wine or bag of grain. There were missing harnesses, missing tools, and missing baubles and beads. Was it possible for one thief, even Gedaliah the Goniff, to abscond with so much in one night? Surely, he had invited fellow bandits from Zamosc and Tishevitz to join him in this burglars' debauch.

Chelmers gathered in the town square. Shopkeepers and store owners lamented and wailed, moaned and mourned. Many of the elders had themselves suffered losses. In such a moment, eyes always turn to the rabbi.

"Rabbi, our night watchman has betrayed us," said Yankel the Tailor.

Reb Feivel shrugged. He turned to Heschy the Night Watchman. "What happened last night?" he inquired.

Heschy shrugged back at the rabbi. "It is true that I watched the thieves break into the shops and stalls. What could I do? I was sitting high on the horse and the horse was firmly fastened to the hitching post. Who would hear me if I called out from there? So, I thought perhaps I should untie the horse and gallop after the thieves. But then I thought, what if the horse should take it into its head to charge into the forest where the wild animals wait for their delicacies? Would I not resemble a nice piece of herring to a pack of hungry wolves? Would it be better for me to be a brave dead man or a wise beggar, I ask you?"

Zelig the Bedecked, the mayor of Chelm, interjected, "Why did you not get down off the horse and run to the shopkeepers' doors, rousing them with cries of 'Thieves! Thieves!'?"

Heschy the Night Watchman cocked his head in thought. He plaintively explained, "My job was to watch while the shopkeepers sleep. If I were to wake them at night, I would be derelict in my duties. So I came to them at the earliest possible moment, before the morning prayers were said."

This is not quite the end of the story. The shopkeepers paid Heschy his watchman's salary for the night before. Then shopkeepers and elders met for seven days and seven nights, sending out for food frequently and downing a serious amount of Chelm's famous plum schnapps. In the end, it was decreed that (1) it was more dangerous to have a night watchman than not to have one, (2) it was more costly to have a night watchman than not to have one, and (3) Heschy the Beggar was preferable to Heschy the Night Watchman.

No one can say that Heschy was not pleased by this. To the contrary, it is said that shortly thereafter, Heschy courted a wealthy widow named Batya who procrastinated, saying she would be too embarrassed to marry a beggar. Undaunted, Heschy made a bargain with her: "Come with me for a week," he said. "Live as I do, as a proper mendicant. If, at the end of the week, you still hesitate, I will no longer beg you for your hand in marriage." The way I heard it, at the end of the week, Batya the Wealthy Widow refused to resume her old way of life. To this very day, you can find the two of them—Heschy and Batya—sitting beside the butcher shop or outside the tavern, pleading for a coin—copper or silver or gold—beseeching a gift, entreating any donation from any passerby—and smiling, laughing, hugging, and kissing when no one is looking.

A TALE OF TWO VILLAGES

✺ The annals of Chelm preserve a story that, while unlikely, may yet be instructive. It concerns a certain Gimpel the Twister who earned his moniker at his employment, braiding hemp into rope. He was married to Rachel Zoshe, who in three years gave him two daughters and four years later presented him with a son.

It happened once that Gimpel the Twister did not arise at his usual time. Rachel Zoshe brought Baby Binyomin to the bed, allowing the baby to pounce on the bed and bounce on his father. "Get up," said Rachel Zoshe.

"Not now," replied Gimpel the Twister, straining to keep his eyes shut. "I am just at the edge of a dream."

"Dream, *shmeam*! The rich lay in bed and dream. The rest of us have bread to knead and mouths to feed—and all the things we do to keep ourselves from our dreams. Get up, Gimpel."

Gimpel opened one eye. "Rachel Zoshe, every day is the same in Chelm," he told her. "Always it starts when Baby Binyomin jumps on the bed and bounces up and down crying for his mama. Zissa and Masha Leah argue. You and I get up. I send Zissa to milk the goat; she claims that it is Masha Leah's turn to milk the goat. I send Masha Leah to milk the goat; she insists it is Zissa's turn to milk it. I get up and milk the goat. You make the breakfast. We eat. I go to the synagogue. I say the prayers wrapped in my tallis, with *tefillin* straps trussed on my arm and dangling from my head. The prayers end. I share a schnapps with the rabbi and the min-yan. I go to work. I braid hemp into rope. I come home. You yell at me that I am late; dinner is getting cold on the table. Zissa and Masha Leah dispute who should serve the dinner and who will clean the dishes. Baby Binyomin is hungry. The family eats. Baby Binyomin is tired. Masha Leah and Zissa disagree about whose turn it is to put Baby Binyomin to bed. You put Baby Binyomin to bed. I fetch enough firewood for the stove to stay lit overnight. We go to bed while Zissa complains she cannot sleep because Masha Leah keeps talking to her. And Masha Leah says that Zissa will not leave off humming long enough for her to fall asleep. The next morning Baby Binyomin jumps on the bed and yells, 'Wake up! Wake up! I'm bored!'"

Rachel Zoshe shook a fist in the air. "Gimpel, Gimpel, I have no time for this. Go! Milk the goat. Breakfast is already on the table."

"Things are different in Lutsk," said Gimpel, turning on his back and opening both eyes to stare at the ceiling. "I hear the sky is clear above Lutsk, not so grey as our sky. And when the sun shines in Lutsk in the morning, birds chirp, dogs yap with excitement, and people sing."

"Go milk the goat. Or tell Masha Leah to go milk the goat. Stop bending my ear with nonsense."

"In Lutsk, the houses are beautiful and neighbors love one another. Oh, yes, people in Lutsk are surely happier than people in Chelm." Gimpel was out of bed now, pulling up his trousers and putting on his shoes.

"Who tells you all this silliness about Lutsk?" Rachel Zoshe demanded.

"I saw it in my dream," said Gimpel. "The dream came three times. I told Reb Feivel, the Glory of Chelm, and he said it is written in the Holy Books, 'The same dream three times—a truthful message.'"

Rachel Zoshe stared at her Gimpel. "*Mazal tov*, congratulations," she said. "Now you know the truth. Get moving."

"Let Zissa milk the goat. I am going to Lutsk," Gimpel announced.

"You have no money to go to Lutsk."

"I will walk."

"Lutsk is far away."

"I will walk to faraway Lutsk!"

"Why?" asked Rachel Zoshe.

"Because it is there!" declared Gimpel the Twister. "And I will not return until I have seen the Great Synagogue of Lutsk with my own eyes."

Rachel Zoshe wondered. Had she ever seen Gimpel so determined before? She knew no one in Chelm who had ever visited Lutsk. She had no idea how far Lutsk was from Chelm, only that it was a long distance. Did she know this Gimpel? Then she thought, "Surely, he will start out and turn back after a while."

She patted Gimpel on his back. "Look at your shoes; they are already tattered. They will wear out long before you reach Lutsk!"

"They are old shoes, true, but still good. Who knows how long they will last? If they wear out, I will wrap my feet with rags and keep walking."

Rachel Zoshe gave up. She sent Zissa to milk the goat and Masha Leah to feed Baby Binyomin. Meanwhile, Rachel Zoshe took some rags she used for cleaning. She made a traveler's lunch of bread and cheese and dried fish for Gimpel. She took sackcloth and folded it around the lunch and the rags, closing the top of the bundle with rope.

Gimpel the Twister kissed Baby Binyomin, hugged his wife, yelled at his two daughters to learn to love one another, threw the bundle over his shoulder, and set off for Lutsk. He knew how to start this journey, he thought. He had to pass through the forest east of Chelm. He did not know what was at the end of the forest. How far would the path take him? If he were lucky, he thought, it might take him all the way to Lutsk.

He had walked the forest path for a few hours when he remembered Rachel Zoshe's warning. He stopped and removed his shoes. He took the rags from his bundle and tied them around his feet. He knotted the laces of his shoes together and wore laces and shoes like a tallis, with one shoe dangling on each side of his chest. The shoes he would need when he reached Lutsk.

Twice, travelers passed him, but neither spoke to him. One was carrying wood toward Chelm. The other was hurrying along toward Lutsk. But Gimpel the Twister could not hurry. With rags on his feet, he had to pick his way around pine cones and acorns and stones poking up from the ground. He tried to walk only on the softer carpet of fallen leaves and nettles. His eyes were trained constantly on the ground, guiding his feet.

He had no idea how far he walked. He seemed alone in a world of trees and branches with light that broke through occasionally here and there in patches. He did know that it was growing darker. The day was coming to a close and soon it would be too dark to see the path.

He looked for a likely site and spied an opening where a dead tree trunk had fallen. He could sleep in the branches of that trunk and not fear the animals that roam the forest at night. So he stopped there and ate the "lunch" that Rachel Zoshe packed for him that morning. As he ate, he considered his journey. The forest was dense. He had hardly seen the sun all day. What if he could not see the sun when he awoke? How would he know the right direction to walk?

He was tired and would have to sleep soon, so he thought, "I will place my shoes on the path and point them in the direction of Lutsk. When I awake, I will go in the direction they are pointing."

This would have been an excellent plan if chance had not intervened. Chance, though, has a champion in Heaven. As Gimpel the Twister slept blissfully in the stout branches of the fallen tree, a wolf—dark brown with grey markings on its sides and a grey tail—came along and spied Gimpel's shoes on the path. Smelling the shoes, the wolf decided they might make a meal. He picked them up in his powerful jaws by the knotted laces and was about to make off with them when a second equally hungry wolf—grey as nightfall with socks of brown—stood in the path and snarled, challenging the brown wolf for his booty. The brown wolf dropped the shoes to better growl at the grey wolf and the two faced off as if they were about to fight to the death over Gimpel's shoes.

At that instant, a squirrel dropped out of a nearby tree. The two wolves spied it, abandoned their grim contest, and both charged after the squirrel. For its part, the squirrel zipped this way and that in search of a low-hanging branch, the two pursuers close behind. What happened to the squirrel, the brown wolf, and the grey wolf need not concern us. What happened to the shoes is a matter of deep import. When the brown wolf dropped the shoes—the odds had been fifty-fifty, but as destiny would have it—the toes of the shoes landed pointing toward Chelm.

In the morning, Gimpel awoke, eager to resume his journey. He bragged to himself, "How wise I was to place the shoes on the path to point me the way to go on! For now it is obvious that I would have no other way of knowing whether to take the path to the right or to the left." So saying, he threw the shoes across his shoulders and set out in the direction the toes had been pointing.

He walked for hours. His stomach was growling, but his spirits did not sag. His dream coaxed him onward to the city of Lutsk. Surely, he would reach it before nightfall. His feet were sore from walking in rags; his eyes were trained on the path; his imagination was fixed on what he was bound to see. So he passed nearly the entire day.

Suddenly, he saw it before him: The wall of the city of Lutsk! "Behind that wall," he thought, "I will see such sights as no one from Chelm has ever seen." He paused only long

enough to put his shoes back on his feet. He was ready for his
great adventure.

He came to the city gate and here he encountered the
first marvel. A man who looked just like Zalman Shelomo the
Gatekeeper of Chelm was sleeping just inside the gate. Gimpel the Twister thought, "This is remarkable. Is every city
gate guarded by a man who looks like Zalman Shelomo? Or is
it only the village of Chelm and the town of Lutsk that have
such a one?"

Inside the walls, the city of Lutsk unfolded before his
eyes. It was almost dusk, the time when shadows and light
mingle. The outlines of the town were delineated in bizarre
and wondrous fashion. How the houses, the shops, and the
streets seemed foreign, and yet familiar! In one glance, he
thought, everything was different from Chelm. But in another glance, he thought, Lutsk and Chelm were much alike.

He smiled at a man who looked a lot like Yankel the Tailor. "*Shalom aleichem*," the man greeted him. He politely
replied, "*Aleichem shalom*," glad to be received in such a familiar way by this stranger. Then he came near the tavern
and other strangers also greeted him. And each stranger bore
a resemblance to someone he knew from Chelm. That woman
passerby looked like Raisel the Matchmaker. That man sitting beside the tavern looked like Zev the Treasurer of Chelm.
He headed toward the center of town, ready to catch his first
glimpse of the famous Great Synagogue of Lutsk.

Lo and behold, the Great Synagogue of Lutsk looked like
the synagogue of Chelm. But of course, he told himself, this
was bound to be true. A synagogue in one place is always like
a synagogue in another place. And this Great Synagogue of
Lutsk was obviously larger and more beautiful than the one
in Chelm, even if they looked the same from the outside.

Then he thought, "There is more to all this than meets
the eye, for the streets of Lutsk are laid out almost precisely
as the streets of Chelm. If I turn this corner," he thought, "I

will be close to where my home would stand if this were Chelm and not Lutsk." So he turned the corner.

Now he was doubly mystified. A house that looked just like his house stood directly before him. He stopped and listened. He could be mistaken, but it sounded like the voices inside were the voices of his own daughters, bickering. He even thought he could hear a baby like his own Baby Binyomin crying.

"I must investigate this," he said to himself. But as he approached the house, a woman called to him from the doorway. "At last you are here. Come in," she said wiping her hands on her apron. "Your dinner is waiting on the table."

He was aghast. The woman could be Rachel Zoshe's twin sister! Or else, there must be a second Rachel Zoshe in Lutsk, the way there was a second Zalman Shelomo at the gate of Lutsk. And who could she be calling to? Was there a second Gimpel the Twister in Lutsk, too? And where was that other Gimpel, seeing that it was time for dinner? Had he gone away to investigate Chelm, the way Gimpel had gone away to investigate Lutsk? If so, was it not only proper for this Gimpel to take the place of that Gimpel, if only for a dinner? After all, he was famished from his long journey to Lutsk. What harm would it do for him to eat at the other Gimpel's table?

As soon as he stepped into the house, an exact duplicate of Baby Binyomin fairly bounced into his arms. The two daughters of the Gimpel of Lutsk looked and squabbled like duplicates of Zissa and Masha Leah, the daughters of Gimpel the Twister of Chelm. The borscht the Rachel Zoshe of Lutsk brought him tasted just like his wife's borscht.

Then the wife of the Gimpel of Lutsk asked, "How was your journey, Gimpel?"

He nearly jumped out of his skin. The name of her husband was the same as his! Could her name be the same, too? He tried it out: "It was a long journey, Rachel Zoshe."

The woman did not blink an eye. She said, "You must be tired."

"Yes," he answered. And automatically, he added, "I feel a bit homesick, too. I wish I were in Chelm."

"What then?" Rachel Zoshe asked in surprise. "You are in Chelm, and we are in Chelm, so you have no reason to miss us."

That was when Gimpel the Twister understood the plain truth, which surely will come as no surprise to you, dear reader. Here is what Gimpel the Twister of Chelm reasoned:

"As everyone in Chelm knows, Chelmers are particularly wise, while people outside of Chelm tend to be more foolish. No doubt, the people of Lutsk admired the people of Chelm so much that they built their town to look like Chelm. made matches of husbands and wives to match the wise matches made by Chelmers, named their children to match the names Chelmers gave to their children, and so on. In short, they patterned everything in Lutsk after everything in Chelm just to pretend they were as wise as the Chelmers. They did not even realize that Chelmers called their town Lutsk! They called their town Chelm."

So Gimpel the Twister made a decision: "I will live here in Lutsk," he told himself, "and pretend that I am living in Chelm until such time as the Gimpel of Lutsk returns. When he returns, I will return to Chelm. If he never returns, I will live in Lutsk forever and pretend, along with all the other Lutskers, that I am in Chelm! The best thing about this arrangement," he thought, "is that I will now be the wisest man in Lutsk!"

When morning came, Baby Binyomin jumped on the bed and bounced up and down crying for his mama. Zissa and Masha Leah were already arguing. Rachel Zoshe demanded that someone milk the goat. He called to Zissa to milk the goat. Zissa complained it was Masha Leah's turn. The girls vied with one another as Gimpel dressed, went out, and milked the goat. Gimpel left for the synagogue where he gave thanks for all the blessings that were his. And just before the prayers ended, he whispered, "O God, let the Gimpel of Lutsk stay among the wise folk of Chelm as long as he wishes. I am satisfied here among the foolish folk of Lutsk."

ANY DAY NOW

✱ The shammes of Chelm was aging. Parts of his job he still did well, while other parts were increasingly difficult. Reb Feivel, the Glory of Chelm, had been rabbi for quite some time. In the beginning, the shammes had assisted him as a shammes should. Nowadays, Reb Feivel often assisted the shammes.

Micah David the Brewer was a regular at morning prayers in the synagogue. One time, Micah David finished praying, downed his shot of morning schnapps with the other regulars, keeled over, and died. Reb Feivel stayed with Micah David's corpse until Chelm's official burial society could be notified to remove the body and prepare it for proper burial. In the interim, Reb Feivel asked the shammes to go to the home of the late Micah David the Brewer, may he rest in peace, and inform his wife Tzvia that her husband had passed away. Reb Feivel cautioned the shammes, "Mind you, break the news to her gently."

As the shammes walked to the house of Micah David, may his memory be for a blessing, he thought about the best way to tell his widow. Perhaps it would be less painful for her if she thought her husband had died in some noble fashion, not after downing a glass of schnapps. Should the shammes say that her husband died reciting the standing prayers, dropping dead while praising God? Should he say that the good man Micah David, may his soul rest with God, had managed to whisper a final message of love and concern for his beloved Tzvia, wishing her well, begging her to be comforted?

As he was ruminating on the most considerate way to inform Tzvia, he arrived at her house. He knocked and she opened the door. Face to face, the shammes forgot all the agreeable things he planned to say and began formally, "I have been sent by the rabbi to see the widow Tzvia."

"I am Tzvia. My husband is Micah David the Brewer. But I am no widow!"

"If I were you," the shammes replied, "I wouldn't bet on that."

This questionable interaction caused much commotion. Reb Feivel spent a long time apologizing to the widow Tzvia.

The shammes spent a long time apologizing to Reb Feivel. He had been confused, the shammes admitted. He had truly meant to do better.

Reb Feivel spent a long time forgiving the embarrassed and upset shammes. "Anyone could make a simple mistake," Reb Feivel said. "Let me make you feel better."

"How?" the shammes asked.

"I'll tell you a shammes story about a simple mistake. Here is how it goes:

"A man from Brisk went to visit the synagogue in Lvov, and the shammes there entertained the Brisker with a riddle. He asked the Brisker, 'Guess who it is—he is my father's son, but he is not my brother. Who is it?'

"The Brisker tried in vain to answer the shammes' riddle. Finally, he said, 'I give up. Who is it?'

"The shammes of Lvov laughed and said, 'It is I, of course!'

"The Brisker returned home and could hardly wait to test out his new riddle. In the tavern, he challenged his friends, 'Let me put a riddle to you all. Let us see who among you will be the first to answer it. Here's the riddle: Guess who it is—he is my father's son, but he is not my brother. Who is it?'

"His friends were clueless. At last, they said, 'Tell us the answer. Who is it?'

"The Brisker grinned triumphantly. 'Why, the answer is obvious,' he said, 'it is the shammes of Lvov!'"

The shammes of Chelm laughed, his heart warmed by the rabbi's story. He felt a little better.

Nevertheless, Reb Feivel was concerned. The High Holy Days were approaching. Before they arrived, the shammes would be faced with an arduous task. Each year, on the Sabbath before the High Holy Days, prayers of penitence were offered at midnight. Traditionally, in the hours leading to midnight, the shammes would walk through the whole village, knocking on every shutter, calling Chelmers to the synagogue for the midnight prayers. Reb Feivel foresaw that this year the walking and the knocking would be too much for the old shammes.

Reb Feivel brought the matter to the elders at the Town Hall. He asked them, "How can we make the shammes feel like he is still doing his job but without allowing him to walk in the cold to knock on every shutter in Chelm?" The elders discoursed, debated, and devised. Plan after plan was brought forward and rejected. Food was ordered. Then, true to their nature, on the second day of deliberation, they formulated a plan agreeable to all. They called it the Walk Nowhere Plan. Carrying out the Walk Nowhere Plan was left to Zelig the Bedecked, the mayor of Chelm, since he owned drays and work horses, and he could hire draymen to do the job.

On the Friday afternoon before the High Holy Days, three drays pulled in front of the synagogue and Zelig's draymen set to unloading them. The shammes and the rabbi heard the banging and came to see what was happening.

"What are these?" the shammes asked the draymen.

"These are shutters," one of the draymen answered.

"Ho! That I can see. But the synagogue does not need new shutters, and no synagogue could ever use so many," the shammes protested.

"These shutters are not for the synagogue, dear friend," Reb Feivel explained to the shammes. "Zelig the Bedecked, our esteemed mayor, on behalf of the elders, has sent his draymen to remove one shutter from each and every house in Chelm. Instead of you going from house to house tomorrow night to knock on shutters, the elders have delivered the shutters to you. Now, you can knock on the shutter of every house in Chelm without leaving the synagogue!"

Despite the Walk Nowhere Plan, the season of the High Holy Days demand constant toil for rabbis and their assistants throughout the Jewish world. By the end of the Day of Atonement that year, with still more than a week of holy days left to go, the shammes of Chelm was ambling from morning to night, from task to task, like a golem, a regular Jewish zombie. Reb Feivel, too, was exhausted from doing his work and also assisting his assistant with his.

After the rigorous holiday season, Reb Feivel returned to the elders of Chelm at the Town Hall and said, "We must seek a new shammes. But before that, we must honor the many years that our shammes has worked for the synagogue and its rabbis. And we must find a way for the old shammes to retire with dignity."

The elders agreed with the rabbi. Yet the puzzle he posed was fraught with intricacies. No shammes in memory had ever retired. (On the other hand, for them, there had been only this one shammes in memory.) The thought of finding a replacement was alarming, but finding a way for the shammes to retire with dignity was daunting. Still, they were the elders of Chelm; it was up to them to formulate a strategy.

The council met for seven days and seven nights. Large quantities of food were ordered and consumed. The elders confabulated, proceeding as they had always proceeded.

Reb Feivel, the Glory of Chelm, took frequent short naps, often rudely interrupted by the sound of his own snoring. Yankel the Tailor would then lean over and whisper in Reb Feivel's ears the current state of the debate.

Sissel made comments like "That plan is as clear as fish balls" or "If your mother knew you think like that, she would have stopped feeding you before you were born." Her interjections tended to be inscrutable to all but Reb Mendel of Apt who often found Sissel so incisive that he would leap to his feet, take up his accustomed stance (in honor of the ancient sage Hillel), and pronounce a hearty, "Aha!"

As if Reb Mendel's "aha" were in Aramaic (the arcane tongue of many a Holy Book), one of the other two sages of the academy of Chelm would interpret what Reb Mendel of Apt had in mind.

When not explaining the meaning of Reb Mendel's "aha," Reb Peretz of Ponder focused his attention on some aspect of the room, some piece of an elder's apparel, or some inner message he alone intuited. Meanwhile, Reb Feibush of Lublin alternately knit his brow—shifting the northern hemisphere of his facial skin upward into what looked like small hills and dry river beds—and raising his right eyebrow—shifting the left crescent of his facial skin downward like a spring runoff on a cliff and sending the right crescent up in miniature pinnacles of flesh.

Zelig the Bedecked, mayor of Chelm, listened, waiting for any inkling of consensus, upon which he would rise and restate the view which had last garnered the upper hand in a stentorian voice to lend it the weight of his considerable authority as mayor.

Tzeitel the Butcher's Wife served as the resident critic, ready to cut the innards out of any proposal in any way flawed, and unwilling (to the dismay of other elders) to replace any proposal she nixed with a suggestion. Tzeitel was fearless but equal-handed, ready to undermine even the mayor himself when he inadvertently supported an insuperable suggestion.

Kalman the Fixer was, perhaps, the most practical. He waited until consultations concluded, until a vote was taken, and then presented himself as the obvious candidate to put into practice the slightest demand of the council. Raisel the Matchmaker thought of herself as one who could hear both sides of an argument and marry them. Dovidl the Nose, a true fisherman, trawled for larger solutions among the schools of smaller answers. Hirschel the Wood Carrier and Naftali the Water Carrier were ever in the heat of any debate, one throwing wood on the fire of a hot suggestion, the other throwing water on the burning embers of a dying resolution.

Zev the Treasurer cared only for fiscal repercussions. He could be counted on to be counting the cost of any proposal in terms of coins in the village purse.

As for Zalman Shelomo, he ate heartily when food was ordered and made any recommendation that might bring Chelm closer to his ideal: somehow becoming three of himself so that he could make a final capture of Gedaliah the Goniff.

This was the council of elders of the village of Chelm, an admirable crew. Yet, one more element should be adduced, for when the elders were together, as they were nearly every morning, they were not just the sum of their several selves, they were more perspicacious than their several selves.

Raisel the Matchmaker rose to speak. "Who ever heard of the poor retiring? That is what marriage is for. As I always say: Marry to have children and when you are old, they will provide for you."

"It is written, 'one father can support seven sons,'" Zev the Treasurer replied, "'but seven sons cannot support one father.' If marriage is to raise children to support us in old age, it is a dismal failure."

"Pity the women more than the men. Men stop working," Tzeitel the Butcher's Wife added, "but women, never."

Sissel agreed and added, "Dying while you are young is a great boon in your old age."

Kalman the Fixer observed, "It is little matter whether marriage is an answer or not. The fact is that growing old in poverty is a blessing. You hardly notice the difference between what you earned working and what you live on when you stop working."

Reb Feivel snored himself awake. Yankel the Tailor confided the state of the discussion. Reb Feivel arose and said, "The shammes never married. He has no children to support him, no wife to care for him. The village has kept him in poverty all his life. Shall we leave him a beggar in his old age?"

One suggestion, offered by Dovidl the Nose, held some promise. "It is well known," he said, "that we Chelmers worry about everything. Worrying is the high price we pay for the wisdom we inherit. Why not pay the shammes to worry for us?"

At first, it seemed an elegant solution. The shammes would have a new job, one he could do without leaving home. But there was a small hitch in the Worry Plan. As Zev the Treasurer pointed out, "If we pay the shammes to worry for us, he will have a steady salary. If he has a steady salary, he will have nothing to worry about. Then the rest of us will have to worry more."

A vote was taken; the Worry Plan was defeated by a narrow margin.

It became obvious that their concentrated effort to solve the problem of retirement in Chelm was as surely mired as an ox in the roadway in the rainy season. As is ever the case, though, the answer the elders arrived at came about in the most oblique way.

Reb Peretz of Ponder had been staring for a very long while at a certain sliver protruding from the edge of one of the floorboards of the Town Hall. Suddenly, he raised his head and announced, "People of Chelm, prepare! Change is in the air! The Messiah is coming!"

Reb Mendel of Apt clambered up to a standing position on his chair, raised his finger in the air, lifted one of his feet in Hillel's posture, and let forth a series of "Aha!"s in varying tones and inflections.

Reb Feibush of Lublin's facial expression changed with each variance of "Aha!" The skin on his face folded and unfolded so rapidly, it produced the oddest impression that his beard, his eyes, his nose, and the hair beneath his skullcap were standing still while the rest of him had come to a rolling boil. He pled with Reb Mendel, "Slower! Reb Mendel, slower! Have mercy!"

Finally, Reb Mendel fell silent, looked around, and appeared amazed at where he found himself. Raisel the Matchmaker grabbed a glass of schnapps and held it to his lips, then helped him down from his chair.

Reb Feibush stood. "Reb Mendel is absolutely brilliant," he began. "We have a new reason to worry. After all, we do not live in Jerusalem, not even in Warsaw or Lublin. Chelm is small. Reb Mendel wants us to consider this very seriously. He says that the Messiah will eventually find us no matter where we are, but the Messiah may not find us—may not even seek us—for many years." At this, Reb Feibush knitted his brow so tightly that it worried Yankel the Tailor who knew the danger of knitting things too tightly. Yankel grabbed a glass of schnapps for Reb Feibush, who drank it, sat in his chair, threw both his legs forward, leaned back, and sighed, allowing the skin on his face to respond to the gravity of the situation.

Reb Feivel, the Glory of Chelm, rose to his feet. "I see a little bird that sees where this is leading," he said, pulling nervously at his beard. "Reb Mendel and Reb Feibush are reminding us that the Messiah might not look for us, but we can look for the Messiah."

Hirschel the Wood Carrier said, "*Nu*, what have our people been doing for all these years if not looking for the Messiah."

Naftali the Water Carrier replied, "Not *looking*, Hirschel; our people have been *waiting*—waiting for the Messiah."

"We can build a tower on the mountain!" said Zelig the Bedecked, mayor of Chelm. "On the tower, we can station a watchman to tell us when the Messiah has arrived."

Sissel nodded her head sagely, observing, "A tall tower sees the world."

Reb Feivel said, "Not the tower, Sissel, but the watchman! The shammes can become our lookout for the Messiah!"

There was a round of applause which Sissel considered a response to her observation. She blushed. "It was just a suggestion," she said modestly.

Zelig the Bedecked, sensing a consensus, put the matter to a vote. "How many are for building a Messiah Tower?"

The Messiah Tower was approved by acclamation. Who could deny the wisdom of this decision? For thousands of years, Jews had been waiting patiently. Now Chelm had invented a way to wait actively for the Messiah. On top of that, the shammes would have an income. It was, as anyone can see, pure genius.

Above Chelm is the mountain, and at the crest of the mountain is the Messiah Tower. Winter, spring, summer, and fall, the shammes made his way to the Messiah Tower and climbed to its top, keeping a sharp eye out for the approach of the Messiah, who was expected any day.

Of course, there came a time when the shammes could no longer climb the mountain, much less climb to the top of the Messiah Tower. The three sages of the academy of Chelm made the shammes a place in the comfort of their school and treated him as a treasured student—in fact, their only student. The shammes imbibed the teachings of the Division of Highbrow Scholarship, the Division of Advanced Amazement, and the Division of Dire Probity. Had he lived, he would have become wiser than all three of the sages combined. Since he had been a shammes so long that no one knew his real name, he was buried with honor, and a headstone was raised upon which was engraved: "IT IS I, THE SHAMMES OF CHELM."

When Avrom the Barrel Maker was too old to craft a decent barrel, he was hired by the elders to be the new watchman of the Messiah Tower. Thus, the issue of retirement in Chelm also found an answer. Avrom, however, came back to the elders after only a few weeks of watching for the Messiah.

"Honored elders," he said, "the work of climbing to the top of the mountain and climbing to the top of the Messiah Tower is not easy on old legs. The truth is, my legs will be more willing to obey me if only you will raise my salary."

Of course, Zev the Treasurer responded first to Avrom's eloquent request. "See here," he told the former barrel maker, "the town treasury is strained at the salary we now pay. But do consider this: the pay may be low, true. But watching for the Messiah is steady work."

In the end, though, a small raise was approved by the elders, but only on condition that while watching for the Messiah, Avrom the Watchman would also keep a sharp lookout from the top of the Messiah Tower for the feathers that were due to reach Chelm any day now.

AFTERWORD:
WHY CHELM?

❋ Right now, in major universities throughout the world—Oxford University (Oxford, England); Harvard University (Cambridge, USA); la Sorbonne (Paris, France); Hebrew University (Jerusalem, Israel); and Dreyacoup University (Tramelan, Switzerland), to name a few—scholars are writing articles and dissertations, conducting seminars, and delving into the origins of the legends and tales that comprise the Chelm canon. The hottest issue of debate among these experts is "Why Chelm?" Why should an otherwise unprepossessing town like Chelm be chosen as the specific locale for such an important *oeuvre*?

What makes this inquiry so attractive to modern scholars is that no unequivocal solution is ever likely to present itself. Hence, the number of doctoral degrees that can be won by investigating "Why Chelm?" is practically limitless; the number of lectures that can be offered to expectant audiences is boundless; and the number of distinguished chairs that may be occupied by those whose research is ever on the verge of ultimate proof is bottomless.

"Why Chelm?" Reams of paper—and, more recently, gigabytes of memory—are lavished on this captivating subject. As for the legendary folk of the legendary Chelm, they are convinced that wisdom is simply Chelm's preordained fate. Their sages say, "Seven degrees of wisdom were apportioned to human beings; six were allotted to the residents of Chelm with the remaining degree spread thinly, like expen-

sive butter on coarse bread, across the rest of humankind."
As for the rest of humankind, however, they are convinced
that Chelm is populated by an unprecedented assemblage of
fools who only believe themselves wise. This implies, of
course, that the question of "Why Chelm?" can be posed as
two questions, to wit: "Why is Chelm the repository of wisdom?" and "Why is Chelm the embodiment of foolishness?"
This added complication is fortunate for Chelm scholars,
since both questions—like the one that spawned them—shall
likely remain forever unanswered.

Little is to be gained by noting that an actual city named
Chelm is located in Poland—that part of Poland which was
also at times located in Russia. The Chelm of Legend bears
no resemblance to the Chelm of Poland. It is only in recent
times that errant authors and romanticizing illustrators
have recreated the Chelm canon in the image of East European *shtetl* Jewry—thereby relocating the nominal Chelm of
Legend to the concrete Chelm of Poland. It was not always so.
The Chelm of Legend, it seems, originated as a Jewish revi-
sion of a German satire lampooning Sir Thomas More's *Utopia*.

Utopia, published in Latin in 1516, depicted a fictitious
island where human beings, left to their own devices, made
consistently wise choices. Around 1550, an anonymous German satirist, responding to *Utopia*, concocted an equally fictitious town named Schildburg where human beings, left to
their own devices, made consistently foolish, unseemly, and
even obscene choices. In Germany, *Utopia* was admired by a
handful of intellectuals, but the low humor of the dystopian
satire propelled it to broad popularity. Before long, the
Schildburg stories were rendered and printed in Hebrew
characters, making them easily accessible to German-speak-
ing, Hebrew-reading Jews.

German Jewish storytellers soon adapted the Schildburg
tales and gave them a Jewish setting. The new Jewish stories
shared elements and even plots with the old German stories,

but they were kinder—discarding the sarcasm, the biting critique, and most of the obscenity. The Jewish tellers had no interest in satirizing Utopia; instead, they turned the lantern of irony inward to expose the bittersweet pathos in their own lives and in the lives of Jews they knew. Their stories flourished among the poorer Jews of Germany and Austria at a time when the Jews of Poland were prosperous and tended to take themselves seriously. Of course, Polish and Eastern European Jews also had folklore at that time, but their tales and legends tended to involve amulets and demons, wonder-working rabbis, and moralizing parables. There is no credible evidence, for example, that the Vilna Gaon or the Baal Shem Tov ever delighted their disciples with an evening of hearty Chelm stories (though, undoubtedly, some scholars are now assiduously seeking precisely that evidence).

It has been suggested that the intention of the German Jewish storytellers was to poke fun at the Jews of Poland. (Well, some will suggest anything.) If this were the case, though, it would come no closer to answering the seed question "Why Chelm?" The Jews of the Chelm of Poland were hardly representative of the Polish Jewish community as a whole. A dozen more iconic choices could have been made by the German Jewish storytellers, including Warsaw. And those choices would not have differed much from other iconic Jewish communities of Eastern Europe at the time, including Vilna, perhaps the archetype of them all.

The German Jewish Chelm stories, stemming from the seventeenth century onward, were revived in the late nineteenth and early twentieth centuries by a talented crop of new Eastern European Yiddish storytellers, including Y. L. Peretz, Mendele Mocher Seforim, and Sholem Aleichem. This reincarnation introduced Chelm to millions of Jews throughout Eastern Europe. As hundreds of thousands of Jews fled persecutions in Eastern Europe, they carried their Yiddish literature with them, spreading the Chelm stories to Israel, England, and the far shores of America. (Sholem Aleichem, for example, who was born Solomon Naumovich Rabinovich in 1859 in a shtetl near Kiev, emigrated to America, died in New York in 1916, and is buried in Queens.) And, despite all this history, still no one could answer the question "Why Chelm?"

To the people of the Chelm of Legend, however, the question "Why Chelm?" is ludicrous. They have always known the answer. The Chelmers explain that wherever Jews settled (or were forced to settle), as soon as a community was established, God provided a cup for that community. Every Jewish community drank from its own cup. The water, the wine, the beer, the schnapps were the same everywhere. What differed was the cup. Just as God creates every human from the same clay, yet every human is unique, so, too, God created every cup of the same clay, yet every cup was unique. Each cup was God's gift, and it determined the singular fate and style of each Jewish community. So the reply to "Why Chelm?" is immediately apparent: The answer is "God only knows."

MEET THE AUTHOR

❀ I am Seymour Rossel. I love a good story (ask anyone) and I have been collecting, writing, editing, publishing, discussing, lecturing on, speaking about, and telling good stories throughout my career. I use stories in my teaching and (as a rabbi) in my preaching. I gifted stories to my children like a legacy of family jewels and now I am privileged to gift stories to my grandchildren. I think *The Wise Folk of Chelm* can be treasured and gifted, especially if the stories are shared out loud.

People I know (even some professional publishers) tell me that publishing has become increasingly difficult—with local bookstores giving way to internet warehouses, reviewers having fewer major outlets, and (so it is claimed) people reading less. I acknowledge these changes but also note some positive ones. Publishing, I think, is becoming more intimate—word of good reads spreads from friend to friend, among family members, and widens through the web. Books can depend less on exaggerated and expensive advertising and more on merit. And new opportunities exist for interaction between author and readers.

So I invite you to discuss your Chelm experience with me. You can find a formal biography of me at Wikipedia. You can reach me by email from my site *www.rossel.net*. And you can friend me in all the usual places. Let's share some good stories.